Mirror

....

Heather Morris

Contents

Prologue

Birthdays weren't a hug deal in our family, but I wanted it to be one. In a week's time, it was my younger brother Kenji's birthday. But as much as he loves gifts, or rather the act of receiving one, he wasn't too keen on surprises so I decided it would be best if I just took him with me for some birthday shopping. That way he can choose what he really wants, and I don't have to use extra energy deciding on a gift that he may potentially never like, although he would never say that. He was too nice like that.

"You did say you will get me anything I want right?" Kenji questions with a knowing smirk on his face. I knew very well that, that smirk on its own earned a lot of keen interest among girls in school.

He's a year younger than me and was the epitome of your golden retriever boy. Bright, goofy, loyal, and just a presence you naturally feel comfortable with. Many even commented that we siblings were the golden retriever siblings given that we both share a similar happy positive approach to life despite the side of the world we live in. Yeah, couldn't say there was much brightness in an underworld.

"As long as it's within my budget, yes." I reply as we both walk along the footpath.

"And how small is that budget?"

"Small? People normally ask how large it is, I'm upset you think I only have a few dollars." I say pretending to be offended, planting a hand onto my chest.

"Daddy's money?" He moves his brows up and down in that annoying but hilarious way. I swear to god this kid.

"Rich coming from you." I retort back, ruffling his dark brown hair we both share. He was turning 15 and he was already way taller than me. I had to go on my tippy toes to reach his head. It wasn't fair he had the tall genes, and I didn't.

He laughs at me for being on my tippy toes before I throw in a joking punch. I know it doesn't hurt because I put very little force into it, but he pretends like he got the worst ever blow by halting on the spot and bends down, wrapping his arms around his waist.

"That hurts, Kaya, I think I deserve two birthday presents." He pouts. If he had done that to our mother it would have worked wonders but it will definitely not work on me.

"Absolutely not." I say and he chuckles. It was also this smile all the girls were head over heels for. The charming one. The alluring one. Too bad he only had an eye for one particular girl. A girl who seems to ignore all his calls and give the side eye. What Kenji doesn't know is that she actually does like him. Watch me be their cupid.

It was an unusually warm autumns day, and we chose to walk over to the mall. It was going to become way too cold for walking this distance soon enough. Got to take advantage of it when and where we can. We both kick through the pile of neatly gathered leaves, probably being a public menace but we couldn't care less.

"So, what did you want?" I ask as I kick through another pile of leaves. There was something that brings satisfaction in this action and there would be no stopping me.

"I actually haven't thought it through. Might just wander around and choose something that peaks my interest." He gives me a grin. I knew that grin very well, he was plotting something. Something I knew would break my bank.

"Hm okay." I reply telling myself I'll chew him out when we start looking around, when I hear a rumbling of a car. I don't think much of it and just kept walking down the pedestrian footpath, but Kenji switches his spot with me so that he was on the side that was closest to the road.

"Wow, how so kind of you. I hope you'll do that to your future girlfriend." I comment and he groans like the mentioning of such thing was blasphemous. He knows that I know about this girl and I will annoy the hell out of him about it. What? Older sister duties.

The rumbling of the car creeps closer, the noise louder.

"You're not going to let go are you?" He comments shaking his head.

"Nope." I pop the 'p' sound just to annoy him all the more.

Screeching of tires hit my ears as the car crept closer.

But we failed to realise that it was speeding. Going miles over the speed limit. We failed to realise that the car itself was swerving or that it wasn't driving in a straight line.

I only realised in the split second before my life shattered. Right in front of me.

Kenji immediately used his body as a shield for me.

I should have been the one to protect him. I was the older one. I was the one who should've been the one to risk my life for him. Not the other way around. But I was rooted in the spot. And I didn't move.

I didn't even attempt to move.

But he did. Kenji did. To protect me.

The only thing I could remember was the car heading towards us. The impact. Glass shattered and split. Blood.

Lots of blood.

Blood on the car. Blood on the road. Blood on me.

Blood on him.

I also remember snapping back into reality, shaking Kenji.

"Kenji, Kenji." I say, in pain. I didn't know what was painful. Everything was.

Kenji's eyes don't open, and I become even more agitated. I shake him harder, call him out louder. His eyes don't open but thankfully, his lips do.

"Kaya . . . t-take care of Mom and Hikari." He whispers out in agony.

"No, no. You have to be with me." I deny his words. I wasn't going to accept such request.

"Don't trust Dad." He continues but I don't hear him.

"Kenji, open your eyes. Kenji you need to open your eyes, please." I beg.

"I love you Kaya. Thanks for . . . being the best . . . sister I could ask for."

And then his lips close. I shake him again. Hard as I could, gritting my teeth from the pain. I yell out his name as loud as I could. But he never responds.

I scream and scream . . . and scream.

I don't know how long we were there for. Me on the floor, Kenji on top of me. I don't know how much blood we each lost. I don't know when the driver died. I don't know when I lost conscious.

I don't know when Kenji was stripped away from me.

But when I woke up next, Kenji wasn't on top of me.

He was gone.

Gone, gone.

His warmth gone.

His free attitude gone.

His smiles gone.

His presence gone.

He was . . . gone.

And I lost a part of myself.

And I would never retrieve back that part of me ever again.

Chapter 1 - Kaya

T his sucks. It sucks a lot.

But I had no right to complain, and bad thoughts were bad thoughts. They shouldn't have a place in my head. Think positive thoughts. Summon them.

Do this for Mom. Do this for Hikari. Do this for . . .

It could've been worse. A lot worse.

As the traitor's eldest daughter, I could have been slapped with the sentence of death, or worse, watch as the rest of my family die before me.

But the Oyabun - the Leader of American Yakuza Organization granted mercy and had left our family alone. The only thing they stripped away was the money my father had made profit from the organisation, which was fair.

It wasn't my father's money, and it certainly wasn't mine or my family's. I wanted nothing to do with the money that wasn't earned rightfully, although that can be up for debate with this side of the world being illegal and all.

How my father planned and conducted kidnapping and attempting murder on the Oyabun's daughter was a thought I could never understand or process fully. He was seen as the most loyal man in the organization but now it was clear he was treacherous.

Greed. That was his motive.

I can't believe I was related to that man.

But then again, it seems my younger brother Kenji knew there was something wrong with him. But he was intuitive like that while I am clueless most of the time. I was pathetic, stupid, and clearly blind to my surroundings.

Taking in another breath and slowly exhaling it out, I square my shoulders and plaster on the best happy smiling face I've learnt to perfect before sliding the blindingly white hospital door open.

"Hi Mom." I greet cheerfully as I close the door walking over to her bed and take a seat that was situated directly next to it.

"Oh my, this is a nice surprise. How are you Kaya?" My mother asks as she watches me get in my seat.

My mother was a soft, quiet natured woman. She had the softest colored brown eyes and equally light brown hair. But with the chemotherapy she had been undergoing, she decided to shave it all off. Now, her hair was replaced by beige colored beanie.

"Good. Same old same old." I reply. "How are you feeling Mom?"

"Not bad myself. You know, Hikari visited a couple hours before you."

Yes, because I forced her to.

"Really? That's nice. I promise we'll come together sometime soon." I reply but I wasn't sure if I'll ever come with my younger sister. We were polar opposites and barely tolerated each other.

It hadn't always been like this. There was a point in time in which she would see me as her role model. The good older sibling. The best older sibling.

But after my Kenji died everything turned sour. My father being a traitor wasn't helping either. And what made this situation even worse was the occupation I had taken.

Unlike me who didn't ever really mind being part of this side of the world, my younger sister, Hikari hated it. And I couldn't blame her. That was the worst part. No matter how much I wanted to hate her, rage at her, scream at her, her points were valid.

Kenji died because of me. My father may have chosen to do what he did because of me. I was at fault for maybe everything . . .

"That would be very nice." My mother murmurs and I snap back to reality. She says that with loving eyes, but I know those affectionate eyes weren't for me. They haven't for a long time.

Well, I was the daughter that stole her son after all.

"I got these flowers for you." I say as I bring up the orange tulips I had bought from the florist this morning.

"Oh my, they look lovely." She admires as she takes in the flower's beauty. She had always enjoyed flower arrangement and looking at flowers made her content.

"I'll go put them in vase and put water in it too." I say before standing up, finding the unused vase from the small closet with her belongings in it and walk out of her room.

Leaning against the wall outside, I breathe out another sigh . . . this time, out of frustration. It is so suffocating in there. Despite the sufficient supply of oxygen, I feel as though I am being asphyxiated. No amount of oxygen seemed to be enough.

No. Don't you dare think like that. She is your mother. You can't blame her for the way she thinks. Everything is your fault anyway. You have no right to think that way.

Taking in another deep breath, I calm my thoughts and march away to find a sink and fill the vase with it.

I wish I could drown in water . . .

Yeah, the last time you did that, he got you out and pretended like nothing ever happened.

Shoving the thought away, I place in the soft orange tulips into the vase now filled with plenty of water and begin my walk back over to my Mother's room.

Just a couple more minutes I chant to myself. Just a little bit more.

I approach the door when I hear my mother's voice talking. Who was she with?

"It's so nice to see your face again. Ryo - san, I'm . . . I'm so sorry for what had happened."

"You don't need to apologize. My father and myself are aware that you and the rest of your family have no direct involvement in it and Minori has no resentment towards your family. Besides, your daughter is doing well to pay the price."

It was him. It was his voice.

Why was he here though?

"I am just worried that what my daughter is doing isn't enough. And seeing that I am in this position . . . I am so, so sorry."

Of course. She was worried that I wasn't good enough. Because to her, I was never enough.

Not good enough. Never good enough. Will never be good enough.

"Your daughter is good enough, in fact, she is great. Her work has been one of the best. You shouldn't concern yourself with that matter. You should be proud of her. We had offered to pay for your hospital bills, but she firmly refused and with her work, your bills are being paid. I understand Hikari-chan is bright, but Kaya is also quite bright if you look carefully."

"I know she is very bright. Always happy and smiles."

"I'm not talking about her personality; I am talking about her intelligence and her worth."

"Oh, of course." My mother says, hesitantly. "Yes. I understand. She does work incredibly hard."

"If you do understand, then that is all I have to say. Please take care of your health."

And then the door slides open, and I come face to face with him.

Him with his pitch-black hair like a crows and dark brown eyes that almost appeared black. Those eyes that stare into your soul. Good thing he didn't really have to analyse me like he did with every other person. He probably knows more about me than myself.

And his stature that towers over me. Like it had always been. It should be intimidating. The operating words being 'should be'. But it doesn't. It never has.

All I feel is ... connection. The need for him to recognize me and my existence.

"Are you going to stand there all day?" Ryo-, I mean Ryosuke-san asks.

He's no longer just your childhood friend. You're not even his friend. There's only one person that he considers as a friend. You are not that person. You were always a constant annoying presence. He is your boss now.

"I apologise." I murmur before sliding over so he could leave.

But even after I move out of the way, he doesn't move. His gaze, fixed on me.

"Just letting you know, you'll probably have work this evening. One body. I'll try not to make much mess out of it."

"Oh, um, I understand." I reply before plastering on a formal smile. Just keep smiling and summon any form of positive emotion. If you think it's real, it will appear like it's real. Then, he wouldn't be able to find out what goes underneath.

It worked. He walks away to leave. But the emptiness I feel after his presence disappears, hurts more than it should.

Normally, all I felt was ... nothing. But with him, just being close to his presence made me feel ... like I was living.

If a Time Machine were to exist, I wanted nothing more than to return back in time when I was a naive little girl. Maybe around 6 or 7 years in age, with nothing on my mind besides what I was going to eat for dinner and how I would spend my afternoons with him and his best friend Kaito, as we ran around his home, playing all sorts of games and just be free.

But reality was a cruel thing.

Our minds were a cruel thing.

And our happy past would never continue into our future.

Chapter 2 - Kaya

- -

T rue to his word, the scene wasn't too bad.

The body was already disposed of and all I had to do, was discard all evidence. Clean with the right products, with the right amount, with the right amount of time.

Being efficient was key, but being meticulous was far more crucial.

Cleaning was never a problem for me. It took my mind off the storm that coursed through my head and my body continues to systematically work my way down to clean the site.

To be honest, blood wasn't something I was always comfortable with. Especially as a little girl, a small scrape of the knee with even the slightest amount of blood and I was crying my eyes out. But when you're surrounded by two boys who constantly fought with each other with the aims to increase their physical power and strength, you slowly get desensitized to it. Not to mention that it wasn't only them who fought. Ryo's- I mean Ryosuke-san's younger sister, Minori-san was also doing sparring sessions with them and even learnt to shoot with arrows and bullets. Yes bullets. Not just guns but rifles too.

She also killed my father by decapitating each of his limb as well as his head.

But I didn't care. I didn't feel anything when I was told the story from Kaito. I didn't feel sick or sad. I was happy. I never really truly cared about him and he never truly cared about me either.

Regardless, it was safe to say blood was a constant factor in my life living with them.

Placing gloves on my hands, I begin to wipe the blood spill with absorbent wipes before I create a mixture with bleach and water. Once the mixture is created, I generously pour it onto the bloodied site and let it sit there for 20 to 30 minutes or so.

During the wait time, I continue to clean around the area, not too much to make it look like everything was sparkling clean, but enough so it looked somewhat natural. But then again, all the dust was cleaned off so it looks suspicious anyway but the upper people worked with that with the police so everything is put under cover.

Noticing the bleach time was finished, I begin to wipe away the bleached content and clean the rest. After this, my for the night was done.

"You're already done?" A voice echoes through the room.

"Ah shit!" I squeal, not expecting anyone to be coming in, let alone talking to me. "Sorry, I didn't mean to, I uh..."

"Are you finished?" He questions once again, leaning against the wall, ankles crossed, dressed in a suit, minus the jacket with his sleeves rolled up to his elbows revealing a little of his irezumi tattoos and veins. Those goddamn tattoos, they were a liability.

"Um, almost yes. Why?"

He doesn't respond, but he taps his fingers against his arms and even though I can't physically hear it tapping, I can hear it tapping. The constant drumming when he is thinking. His habit.

Many say that Ryosuke Sakurazuki can't feel. Have no emotions. Apathetic. And for the most part, that was true. However, what they don't know was that he hides and drowns out all emotions. Because logically speaking, emotion never help in finding solutions.

He learnt to suppress and discard emotions and opted to analyse other people's emotions and worked and acted accordingly.

That was the problem. He had solutions to every scenario, case, problem. I acted on emotions, and nothing has ever worked out the way I wanted it to.

No matter how respected I was a few months ago, I was the traitor's daughter. No matter how hard I worked for my mother and sister, I was a disappointment. No matter how much I want to end my life and just be with it, my emotions, and the voices in my head scream at me to keep going because I needed to take care of my mother and sister. Because that was what Kenji told me to do. To take care of them.

As someone who was involved in taking his life, the least I could do was continue what he had asked for. Even if it's for a short period of time.

"You're disappearing again."

I snap back and return my attention to him. Again, this was the problem. He can recognise everything.

"And you don't have solutions." I shot back. Probably not the best choice of words given that I no longer held such position to talk back but it was out of instinct. A habit I needed to lose real quick if I wanted to survive for the sake of Kenji and my mother and sister.

He pushes off against the wall, slowly, majestically, like he owned this whole place. Truth be told, he did. Own this whole place I mean. He had this way of owning places. It didn't matter where he was, he owned it.

He walks over towards me, taking his time. That was his favorite thing to do, taking his time. It made people feel unsettled, confused. Feel fear. And unfortunately for me, that was what I was exactly feeling.

"You can pretend to the world that you're the brightest girl out there with your fake smiles and kind words, but you will never be able to deceive me. Because in reality, that organ people like to use in a metaphorical sense is already broken apart so bad no taping or glue can fix it." He says as he points at my heart. "Your mind with the voices in your head will keep telling you that nothing will work out the way you want and slowly you'll wither away like flowers when it nears summer and no one close to you, will witness it. But I will. I will watch as you lose yourself and still pretend like everything is fine. I will watch as you physically crumble apart and disappear. I will watch every second of every minute as you disappear. Keep that in mind."

And then he backs away from my personal space and leaves. Like saying such thing was a normal part of his daily life.

The worst part was, besides the part he announced he will take his leisurely time to witness my downfall, he was right. I was falling. Falling without anyone to soften the blow. I was crumbling, with no one to prevent it from worsening. I had voices. Voices constantly telling me I wasn't good enough.

Not Good Enough. Not Good Enough. Not Good Enough. End it. You're a disappointment anyway. No one would care if you disappear. No one wants you here anyway. Who cares? No one cares.

Stop. Stop. Stop! Stop!

"STOP!" I scream to myself, my voice piercing as it echoes against the walls. Haunting my own ears.

I breathe out heavily, closing my eyes, trying to calm myself down.

For the life of every god that exists calm the hell down and stop shaking. Stop being so pathetic.

Just until Mom can get back on her two feet. Just until Hikari graduates high school.

A few more weeks. Just a little more.

Then. . . then. . . then, you can end it. Then you can say you fulfilled what you promised with Kenji.

Just a little more. Just . . . a little more.

Chapter 3 - Ryosuke

Humans are generally speaking, a disappointment.

There are only few people in my life I don't mind being surrounded by. Kaito, my right-hand man, my sister Minori, my mother and for the most part, my father.

And Kaya, for reasons even after two decades of trying to analyse and understand I still didn't understand why.

She was different from anyone else I have ever met. Whether that was when I had first met her when we were three years old, or when she changed into someone else completely nine years ago or now.

If I could, I would grab the three-year-old Kaya back and somehow take out her persona and insert it into the current Kaya. Three-year-old Kaya may have been annoying with her constant chatter and asking useless questions every chance she got, but she wasn't fake. She didn't have blank eyes. She never looked like she was in constant pain that can't be eased with pain killers.

She looked like Minori when she came out of that disgusting place. Except, unlike Minori who used her bitter cold exterior as a defence mechanism which made her stronger, more resilient, Kaya developed none.

None that was healthy anyway.

When she begins to disappear, her eyes empty, her ears hear nothing from the exterior world and only hear the voices in her head, she stays in that exact same spot, sometimes for a few minutes, sometimes for hours.

She was at a constant battle with herself all the time. And it only worsened as the years went by. Every year without Kenji, her younger brother was a reminder of a life with so much potential lost.

And I was barely there to witness it.

Kaya and Kenji were only a year apart and even to me, he was like a younger brother figure. To her, Kenji was her pillar, her confident, her best friend.

It wasn't her fault that he died, but when the person you should be able to place the blame on, aka the driver dies as well, she became the figure to blame on.

Because she was a liability that Kenji felt the need to protect. If she weren't there, Kenji would have protected himself or tried to manoeuvre himself away from the oncoming car. And all the like with the excuses you'll never know for sure. It was pathetic as it was ridiculous.

What they don't know or refuse to acknowledge was that Kenji didn't protect her out of expectation or obligation. He just did because he loved his sister. He just did because it was pure instinct to protect her instead of himself.

I would have done the exact same thing if that were the case with me and Minori. No questions asked.

However, Kenji was a male. An heir. The better option to survive. Not Kaya. A female. With no real use in our world besides marriage of convenience and as a tool to do business.

And with her father being a traitor, nothing was working in her way.

Her mother didn't understand or know how to appreciate her efforts because she couldn't forgive her for the loss of her son. Her sister Hikari, despised her for what she does.

No one, appreciated her.

No one, liked her.

No one, wanted her.

And she knew that. She was well aware of that.

That was why from nine years ago, she attempted to end her life over, and over again. Whether that was by drowning, overdosing, slitting her wrist, or mixing drugs with alcohol, she tried.

And every time I found her.

I don't know what it is with her or me, but I can sense it when something is fading.

When she was fading.

I shouldn't care. Why should I stop someone who wants to die, from dying?

And yet, I was always there when it was happening. I always found myself resuscitating her, keeping her alive. I hear myself praying that she survive. I find myself hoping for her to live. Pleading for her to survive. That I'll do anything for her to live.

There was something wrong with her existence and there was something concerningly wrong with my conscious.

Even as I walk away from the now cleaned up scene, I hear her scream 'Stop!' and that does something within me. My hands clench and chaos ensues my mind.

She was still suffering, losing a piece of herself day by day. But she stopped trying to die two years ago. Two years ago when her mother was diagnosed with cancer. When her sister was deemed to be of great talent academically.

But that didn't mean she stopped thinking about dying and how to die. You can see it in the way she looks at certain things. When she stares too hard at oceans, lakes, ropes, medications, sharps, chemicals, drugs, guns, weaponry.

Her current circumstance was preventing her from acting out on her urge for now, but that only ever lasts so long. Her mother was dying. She may not know it, but her mother transitioned from stage 3 to stage 4, meaning her cancer was no longer curable. Only treatable. Her sister was to graduate soon and was receiving offers from university and college everywhere. Many with scholarships.

Once her mother dies and her sister graduates, the reason she is here would be gone and the urge to end it all will flow through her with more intensity than ever before.

Five weeks. I had five weeks until her sister graduates. Perhaps a few months until her mother dies.

I told her I'll watch her disappear but that was only when worse comes to worse. I wasn't going to let her die alone. But I have no real intention of witnessing it happen.

I don't know what it is with her, or what the hell is wrong with my own mind, but I will prevent it from happening. I will stop the course of her actions that appears to have already been laid out in front of her.

Something was tied to the both us and like the legend goes, once there is a loose end, all will unravel and fall.

If she goes. I go.

If she dies, so will I.

Chapter 4 - Kaya

Sleep wasn't something that came easily to me.

I was always a light sleeper. I awoke to anything and everything. And it didn't help that when I do sleep, I was reliving that moment in my sleep either.

Over time, my body had adapted itself to live with a few handful hours of sleep. Some days I went without sleeping at all. It was easier that way. Besides, it wasn't like I was going to die because I skipped a few nights of sleep.

So here I was at the top of a hill, observing the sunrise, smoking my stash. If little Kaya saw me right now, she may as well have cried and thrown a temper tantrum. Perhaps she would have a heart attack. Who would've guessed the girl who was strict with rules and lived the stereotypical sunshine persona to the T, was now a drug addict, a substance abuser.

Finding comfort in it.

Finding peace in it.

It was pathetic. I knew that. It was the coward's way out. I knew that. It was what people with aimless lives and no purpose does. I knew that.

I was pathetic. I was a coward. And generally speaking, my life held no value or purpose.

Who cares? I certainly didn't.

Four weeks, two days, a handful of hours.

That was my time limit until my sister graduated and would be starting a life of her own. My mother had started planning to go back and continue her treatment at the comfort of her home. I asked my mother's side of the family to check on her every now and then.

When my sister graduates I will be free. Once that countdown reaches zero, I would end this life once and for all.

I take another drag, filling my lungs with chemicals and feel the effects.

Feel a little lighter, more calm, more stable.

It was one of the few things that made me feel numb in better ways. But it wasn't easy obtaining it. I couldn't get it from my organization for obvious reasons, I couldn't get it from the Russian's due to Minori's influence and I couldn't get my hands on any and all sides of the Italians. I don't even know why in that regard, but this world was always interconnected somehow.

So, I had to pay a little extra and get my hands on them from back alleys where a lot of my job is done. It didn't matter how shitty the quality was, if it does the job, then it does the job.

I was about to take another drag, when my heart rate quickens, my skin prickles, and my drag was stolen from my fingertips.

"How many times do I have to tell you not to take this? Do you not understand what this does to you?" He crushes it within his palm without flinching or reacting. Crazy person.

Of all people, I had to be caught by him. Why can't it be Kaito, his best friend and righthand man or even Minori? Why does it have to be him?

"I do, and that is why I am taking them. I only take small amounts and I never cross the line." I retort before realising once again, I was in no position to do so. If he tells me off, I was supposed to bow my head down and robotically reply yes. That was what was expected of me. I close my eyes, not wanting to see the wrath in his. He may often hide his inner emotions, but I do see them from time to time. Lately, it was usually disappointment.

Not surprising. Nor was it unfamiliar. Disappointment seemed to be everyone's normal when facing me.

But closing my eyes wasn't going to solve the problem. He would just wait until I open my eyes. Might as well open them now.

So I do, expecting the same disappointment in his eyes but was taken back when I find something similar to concern.

No, you're making up things. Why would he even care about you, let alone be concerned for you?

"I can't trust you. Unless you are going to your mother's you will stay with me. Unless I am aware of what you are doing, you will stand behind me. That is an order, Kaya. No excuses." He gets into my face. "Do I make myself clear?"

He was not in his right mind. What the hell was he thinking about?

"I can't just stand behind you. No one trusts me. No one wants me near you, let alone stand behind you." I blurt, equally intruding his personal space. "You can't expect me to just stay with you. No one wants that."

"Then do you have a better solution?"

"I promise I won't cross the line." I say, shaking my head. "You know I have done my job well and I was completely sane. I'm still sane. These don't affect me with a few drags. Just trust me."

His eyes darken, and pierces right through mine.

I messed up.

"How am I supposed to trust you when you continuously decide to leave me?" He begins, his voice increasing in volume. "How am I supposed to trust you after the second time you decided to betray my trust and tried to kill yourself again? Hm? How am I supposed to trust you after each and every time I find you unconscious and on the verge of death?"

He doesn't care. He's only saying that to make you feel guilty. He left you too.

But he's the reason why Hikari and Mom were still living. He's the reason why our family was excused.

"Fine. If the people around you agrees and is fine with my presence, then I'll stay." I say. I was almost 100% certain that there will be people who would disagree and scream and yell saying my family and I weren't worthy of being alive.

They are right of course when it came to me. I didn't even want to live.

"That's where you're wrong. They will listen and follow my demands. Not the other way around." He states, his eyes so sure.

I was screwed more than ever before.

Chapter 5 - Kaya

"What a fine weather today! Can't choose whether to drink tea or to hang myself."

- Anton Chekhov

This is a nightmare.

No, it's better than a nightmare, I guess. At least I'm not hyperventilating or sweating breathless. But it was a different type of nightmare and there were three distinctive qualities about both.

One, I couldn't get out even if I wanted to.

Two, I had no say in whether I wanted this to happen or not.

And three, I have to without exception, experience the worst part of the narrative.

Just like the man said himself, no one raised their concerns with me following him. Well, at least not openly. They all still give me disgusted looks here, and a snide remark there. They will all look at me from top to bottom to analyse and come to the conclusion that I wasn't worth anywhere near him.

It seems like a lifetime ago where I was praised everywhere I went and received gifts just to be on my father's and Oyabun's good side.

These hypocrites.

But I suppose I am one myself.

One may say the public's eyes or gaze was the worst part. It isn't.

His presence was.

A few months ago, I talked over him, talked back at him, yelled, and screamed at him, without a single worry. Because I knew him since we were toddlers. Because I knew him inside out like he does me. Because I just knew him.

But this current situation I was in right now, prevented me from doing . . . anything.

I should just be thankful that my family is alive. I know that. My brain knows that. My logic knows that.

But my body doesn't.

All I wanted to do was shake him, yell, and scream about my worries and concerns. He was the only one who knew about them. He was the only one who had seen everything. All the ugly, disgusting, bloody events of my life.

He was the only one who listened. The one that didn't care about who I really was, or the person I had turned into. He was the only one that cared enough to stay. Really stay.

Until he didn't.

That was the worst part.

But it wasn't like he had a choice.

A naive part of me wants to cave in and just cry. Tell him I am exhausted, and I don't want to do this anymore. See how he would react. At the end of the day, it was always easier to accept reality earlier on than to never know or learn about it when it's too late.

But I was a coward. And explaining what goes in my head was something I wasn't very good at or capable of doing. There was too much going on all at once and then nothing at all sometimes. How am I supposed to explain when I can't even understand myself?

"Kaya what are you doing!?" His voice echoed in my head. Why did it sound like he was concerned? I must be hallucinating.

I snap back.

Oh. Crap. What am I doing?

"I'm so sorry." I begin to apologise, taking out a handkerchief and wiping down the tea I spilt. I am such an idiot.

Kaito also gives me his handkerchief which I take and thank while the man on the opposite side of me gives me a glare. Staring me from top to bottom. Of course.

He was a business partner. And a very good one at that from what I could gather. You knew who did business well. They were those who dressed well, but not flashy rich. It was all smooth linings, and crisp edges. They were those who had polite words for every and any occasion with a slight jab where you don't really expect. They were those who judge you but switch immediately to neutral if you were deemed somewhat important.

Great to know I wasn't one of those people. But even I think the same of myself so, we were mutual there.

"If you'll excuse me. Kaito will continue our discussion in my temporary absence." Ryosuke-san explains in his fake polite manner. His business tone was so fake to my ears but if you didn't know him, it could be categorised as pleasant on the ears. I hated it.

He stands from his chair, and I pretend I don't care and continue to dry the now non-existent tea spillage. But it doesn't last long. He shifts over to me and whispers in my ear to get out.

I do so thinking that my presence was no longer needed, giving Kaito and the business partner my fake radiant smile I had mastered years ago when I realised plastering it on will allow me to fly under the radar.

However, much to my dismay, he too, left the room with me.

He said he'll excuse himself you idiot.

Oh yeah.

"I'm so sorry about that. It won't happen again." I apologise to him knowing that he was probably pissed and may give a lecture. May, because he was a man short on words. He only speaks when absolutely necessary.

Naturally, he doesn't give a reply, but he grabs my hand and I flinch. Not because he touched me, but because only now did my brain register I burnt my hand.

Without a word, he inspects my hand like it was a puzzle piece he had to solve, before he lets go and take my wrist instead, leading me away somewhere in his home.

I've been to his home multiple times. But I hadn't been here in a while. He left for Japan nine years ago and only came back last year. From that time, I've only been in this expansive resort like house twice, and so much of it has changed.

"What are you doing? Where are we going?" I question as we pass by a few doors that probably led to large rooms, each with a purpose for its existence. No room in this house existed for no reason. Each and every room was a designed for a specific purpose.

As per usual, he doesn't answer me and continues to walk along the corridor and turns a left before he opens one of the rooms. It was filled with shelves stocked with things I wasn't too sure what it was. Still holding onto my wrist, he leads me over to a sink that I didn't even know existed and turns on the taps, places my burnt hand under the cool water.

"How do you not realise you burnt yourself?" He questions more to himself than me.

Even if that question was directed to me, I wouldn't have replied. Simply because I didn't know what to reply. That I built my pain threshold from all the times I decided to leave this world for good? Or how I recalibrated my brain to think pain was good when it became a stimulant when I felt like I couldn't feel anything?

From the information I gathered last week, that thought was not a good idea. I shake my head. Maybe a little too dramatically, seeing that he turns his attention from my hand to my head and looks at me like I had another flower growing on top of my head.

But he soon returns his attention back to my hand, still holding onto it, letting the water run.

I could do that alone, I think to myself but stupidly find comfort in knowing a part of him cares and just stay there, letting him take care of it.

So I just stood there, next to him, his hands on mine, running under the cool water. It was like that for the next ten minutes in an oddly comfortable silence before he turns off the taps. Talk about wasting water.

He nods to me to sit on one of the chairs and I do so before he goes off somewhere. I didn't know where. This room didn't exist when I used to come around.

My hand and a bit of my arm was wet so I stood up to look around for some tissues or a towel but from where I was standing, I could find any.

"I told you to sit." He says looking at me like I was a child who couldn't follow simple instructions. To be fair, I never liked being told what to do.

But I sit back down anyway and so does he with a towel and begins to dry my hands with it. Gently I think. Or was my head playing tricks again? It always seems like it is these days. Is that part of withdrawal symptoms? Probably.

With careful, almost gentle movements, he dries my hands before applying moisturiser on top of my burnt hand. His touch was warm and gentle and the weak part of me wanted this moment to last even a minute longer. Maybe even just a few seconds longer.

"Do not hurt yourself again." He looks at me dead in the eye, his facial features hardening, staring me right down. I wasn't sure why or how something so minor as a burn could bother him, but I reply with a curt nod and reply with a simple 'yes' to indicate I understood.

Perhaps that was all he the answer he needed. With that, he simply nods to himself before disappearing once again to what I presume would be to put away everything he brought out. And so once again, I was left alone.

Should I wait for him? Or should I leave and somehow navigate my way back to the meeting room? No. My presence was not something that would look favourable for our position. I've already made a mistake once; I cannot risk it.

But I do look stupid just sitting here. Right?

"We're going to do rounds today." His voice filters through as I shift my attention back to him while he was making leisurely way back to where we seated minutes ago.

Rounds. Which meant clubs. Which meant drinks, music, drugs, and sex. None in that particular order but all of them can be done more than once. With more than one person.

As much as I used to love parties and the festive vibes, my mental capacity cannot take all the stimulation that exists in such place. It was too loud. With too many people. With all different kind of scents. People barging into and smacking into one another with absolute no personal space and blinding lights everywhere.

Well, I suppose what Ryosuke-san does or goes within clubs wasn't really the club itself I guess.

"I understand." I say, dipping head a little lower. People with power liked to feel in power. I wasn't quite sure whether that applied to him because he was more than aware that he had and owned power, but it was best to cover all bases anyway.

"We'll leave around six. I want to get there before it opens."

"Will there be anything you'd like me to do?"

"No. Just stay close."

"I understand." I say submissively knowing that worked like a charm for my father and a few other higher end men of this world. But surprisingly, it never worked for the Oyabun. It was like he knew my fake exterior. He just told me to drop the act and just be who I was. Unlike other people who made a few rude comments there, whenever I exclaimed some rude comment about his son or soldier's, the Oyabun never seemed to mind. In fact he found it amusing and questioned for more information from my perspective.

Today, I realise, his son, also hates my fake exterior. Maybe it was because just like I was used to his indifferent nature, he was used to my upfront chatty nature and wasn't acclimated to my new compliant nature. Or maybe it was because he just despised fake things in general.

Whatever the reason was, his eyes sharpens, his brows knit close, and he looks down at me, before he leans down so we were face to face.

"When it's the two of us, tyou will speak to me the same way you always have." He says before backing away and leaving the room, while I was left standing, sinking in his words.

What did he mean?

Chapter 6 - Ryosuke

New Chapter!!!

Back to Ryo's POV (yayyy!!!). How are you feeling about this story so far? Is it like you imagined?? Do you like the quotes?

I hope you are enjoying and if you want to see more action going on, I promise more things will happen in the near future so please sit tight. More is to come.

But   for   now,   enjoy   this   chapter
☐--

"Tell me where it hurts. Stop howling. Just calm down and show me where."

- Margaret Artwood, The Blind Assassin

Submissive people are unfavourable and dull.

There was no personality or chaos in that. There was no thrill in that. There was absolutely no reason why anyone should be submissive.

Sure, people who work under us should be submissive to some certain extent. I expect them to be compliant and offer their loyalty. I expect them to do what they're told but to also raise issues that can be managed in a more efficient manner. But under no circumstance do I want them to kiss the ground I work

People who desire that aren't built for hard work. They can, however, be the scapegoat when matters turn south. That was the only use they could serve.

Naturally, seeing her being all submissive and looking vulnerable struck a nerve. No, it struck several nerves.

In fact, it pissed me off.

Not a lot of things does that.

Except her. She pissed me off all the time.

Growing up, I've learnt to shut down or tone down multiple emotions and feelings. My father didn't really own them in the first place, so naturally Minori and myself were also missing a few emotions here and there but we were otherwise normal. We just both learnt to rise above emotions.

Well, I did. Not so much my sister or at least not completely.

Initially, I saw that as weakness, but I've come to the realisation that I was glad my sister had emotions. That she was a little more normal than I was. That she could express her emotions when and where necessary.

Regardless, I hated Kaya robotically replying, 'yes sir' and 'I understand." Over and over again. It was ridiculous and nothing like who she was.

Under normal circumstances, she would be throwing a weird look here and some smart comment there. She was far more intelligent than most men I knew and how her brain was able to come up with such colourful words and comments was beyond my understanding of the dictionary or literature. Although I must say, I did prefer tactics, science, and mathematics over literature. It was more conclusive and led to straighter answers.

With the exception of a few variables which can change the whole equation or idea.

In my life, that everchanging variable that I had very little control of was her.

And that was how I liked it.

I enjoyed observing her interesting course of action and unexpected remarks and creating multiple solutions and figuring and deciding which solution was the best (or worst to prolong the situation), and then again, watch her reaction.

However, I couldn't even do that anymore.

She acted in a way that was predictable. Obvious. Boring.

Fucking Annoying.

That was not who she was, and I absolutely despised it.

Not to mention she was definitely slipping away from my grasp and her environment.

Even as I sift through the paperwork in my office room of the building that was thankfully soundproof to ensure that the sound of irritatingly pounding music didn't sift through, she was staring at nothing in particular. No focus. Features empty. Almost like she was hypnotised into nothingness.

Once upon a time, her features were bright. Her light brown eyes shining against the sun or the moonlight. Her lips constantly moving to ask questions and talk nonsense. Her dark brown hair styled into something she saw online and had always managed to compliment her bright features.

But the woman in front of me was nothing like her.

Her light brown eyes were dim. Her pupil size barely changing. Only in light and darkness did they change. They no longer changed through curiosity, awe, or excitement.

She didn't find anything in the world holding such idea.

Her lips were often cracked and dry. I had suspicions she had returned back to her habits of smoking tobacco and weed and a few days ago, I had confirmed my suspicions. She also consumed more alcohol than food, naturally, she has lost a significant amount of weight.

But those things were the things that kept her sane. Or rather the only things that enabled her to drown out the voices in her head.

Her hair was always clean and neat; however, it was always pulled into one. She no longer experimented or attempt to put her long hair into anything else. Practical, but not her.

"Kaya come over here." I order, facing away from her.

She looks up from whatever she was looking at and stares at me. Well, at least her eyes are no longer empty. She hesitates for a second too long before she walks over towards my desk.

"Yes?"

"What did I say about how we communicate when it's only the two of us?"

"I only said one word." She retorts, brows knitted. She was annoyed.

Good. I got something out of her.

"Do this." I command, handing her a pile of paperwork along with a calculator. "Be useful and do some additions will you. Unless you're no longer confident with your mathematical abilities of course."

"I don't need a calculator." She replies, forcefully grabbing the paperwork, with a pen and clutches it to her chest before she walks back to the seating area and set herself to work. Determination plastered on her face.

She always fought for first place in academics when we were younger in school. She always wanted to be first at everything. Realistically, it's not possible to be perfect or number one at everything but she wanted to be one.

She was first in most subjects. Most because science was the only subject I wasn't willing to hand over to her. Until I left of course. Then she was first for every subject.

She was also class president in all years possible until the accident.

She was someone who everyone admired and wanted to be. It didn't matter that she wasn't blond and picture perfect. She had a personality that everyone was attracted to and ruled over everyone. Or in her words, leaded everyone and spoke on their behalf. Same difference.

With her eyes knitted and her attention on all the numbers I had given her, a little bit of her true self shone through. A very miniscule portion but it was something. Naturally, witnessing the old Kaya that I knew and liked had brought a sense of calm I was clearly missing these past few weeks.

Holding onto the calm I currently held within my grasp, I too set myself with the paperwork. Renovation ideas, pricing, thoughts on whether to alter opening times, wages, and the like.

Tedious but put it all together and it created a whole. No piece should go unnoticed or unchecked.

"These don't match up." I look up to find her in front of my desk, two sheets of paper next to each other.

24k. Twenty-four thousand dollars missing. By no means, a significantly large amount but not a small amount either.

"I looked through the other papers, but I couldn't find the missing 24 thousand. Do you have missing papers?"

"No I don't. Someone is moving the money somewhere."

"Are you sure you don't have other papers? Maybe I might have." She looks down, biting her bottom lips. "Or maybe it has something to do with my father?"

No. That report was created three weeks ago and was finalised last week. Minori finished off her father three months ago, meaning 12 weeks ago. It couldn't be her father.

"Kaya, do me a favor."

"A favor?"

"Yes, a favor. Hack through everyone's accounts. They will not go unseen or unpunished."

Chapter 7 - Kaya

N ew Chapter!!! □□□

Another chapter you may have seen from Tiktok, I hope you like reading it.

I should be studying for my exams tmrw but I wanted to post this chapter before it haha. (Pls wish me luck I need to pass this exam□)

Enjoy your reading time.

"You can decorate absence however you want, but you're still gonna feel what's missing."

- Siobhan Vivian

This wasn't right at all.

But I didn't think that way.

I know there was something wrong with me but who knew I was this . . . fucked?

Technology and computer work was something I had always enjoyed but wasn't always good at. It was Kenji who taught me the art of hacking and well, stealing information. Kenji did it to the kids who would bully and torment other kids. He was righteous in a very skewed way. Quite befitting in the world we lived in. In the world I was living in.

But I wasn't using these skills for some righteous reason, not truly.

I was going through each and every single person affiliated to our organization who had access to profit numbers, pricing numbers, wage numbers and well, any numbers. And then match it with their paid numbers.

This process is tedious and for the most part wasted effort. Kenji probably would have known a much more efficient method to find where the missing money went in the first place, but my knowledge was limited and I didn't really want to learn more.

In saying that, I found someone who not only had 24-thousand dollars that was unusually extra to their paid amount, but also an extra 892-thousand dollars that just does not match. Simple logic says that this person is responsible for the money being lost. But instincts said that this was all just a ploy.

"What are you doing?" A condescending voice questions with an edge of disapproval. I turn around in my chair to face her.

"I don't think it concerns you." I reply back looking at my younger sister in the eye.

Hikari was everything I was not.

Intelligent in that genius way, pretty in the idol way, and like her name suggests, bright. Not to me of course, but bright and bubbly towards our mother, her friends, anyone who wasn't me.

"Are you pretending to do the things Kenji used to do? How low are you going to go? How far will you go to pretend you're grieving?" She interrogates, carving out a larger wound somewhere in me.

The urge to breakdown then and there was so violent, I could feel the pressure behind my eyes and my throat tightening, constricting my airflow. But I will myself to keep my composure in check. I cannot cry in front of my younger sister. I cannot show her my weak side.

I may be hurting but she was hurting too. She loved Kenji as much as I did.

Besides, it would be easier for her if she hates me. Facing death and loss was and is easier when you hate the person. If you loved and care about that person, their death could break you – it broke me.

I didn't want that for her.

I'd much rather be hated from her now.

"I'm doing a task for Ryosuke-san."

She puffs out a fake laugh.

"Already trying to be miss perfect? Doing everything you can gain back whatever you had? You know that's not possible. Once I go to uni and graduate, I will take over this family. I will provide for mum. We won't need you!" She leaves and slams the door. The sound loud and echoed in my ears. It's only a sound. It's only one thoughtless action. And yet . . . and yet, it hurts.

Everything in my life seemed like that course of action. Doors shutting in my face.

First it was Kenji. Then it was Mom. Then it was Hikari.

The pressure pressing against my eyes intensifies, and I wipe away whatever was gathering in them. I was so pathetic. So weak and stupid. Why was I crying over this? Why do I feel so insecure and useless in front of my younger sister? She was seven years younger than me for goodness sake.

I turn around to face the screen once again, but I lost whatever concentration I had. There would be no point attempting anything now. I would only mess things up far worse than I have.

Grabbing my keys and phone, I leave my room and walk out the house. Common sense told me I should take the car or at least bring an umbrella. The weather these days had been a miserable mayhem and today was no exception.

The sky was yet to free its tears, but it was grey and cloudy.

But I couldn't care less and begin to jog which then, turned into a run. I run along the path that I have become so used to running over that I didn't even need to think where I was going. My legs took me to where I needed to go.

Within 20minutes, I arrive to the open, large black gates that were oddly comforting and slow myself, so I was walking inside. Taking a familiar route down along the narrow road, seeing names after names after names of people I don't know and would never know of, I arrive at my destination.

"Sorry I came here again, and without flowers. I promise I won't stay for long." I whisper out as I crouch down and run my fingers across the metal words that exists against the grey slab of rock.

Here lies Kenji Hashimoto

1st of October 1999 ~ 24th of September 2014

A thoughtful son and a loving brother

May you rest in Peace

"Can I come over to you soon? I promise it won't be like any other times. Will you come and get me when I do come over to you?"

I wasn't too sure whether he was agreeing or disagreeing to my request, but rain begins to sprinkle down until it started to pour, drenching me wet.

"Is that a yes or a no?"

"Do you ever learn from your mistakes?" His voices hit my ears and I look up realising that the rain was no longer pouring over me.

He was holding an umbrella over me and instead of me getting wet, he was.

"W-why are you here?" I question as I stand up to meet his face. His pitch-black hair now appearing to be even more black if that was even possible. Drops of rain cascaded down his hair and face every now and then, making me realise how sharp his whole face was.

He doesn't answer me. He just stares into my eyes communicating very well that I should've at least brought an umbrella.

I look away from his harsh gaze, unable to keep in contact with them. But as soon as I do so, he takes my chin and pushes it up, so my eyes were meeting his once again.

"You will not look away from me again." He grabs my arm immediately after his comment and begins to pull me out of the cemetery and pushes me inside his car, clicking the seatbelt in place.

"What are you doing? Where are we going?" I stammer out confused.

In his usual fashion, he doesn't give me a reply and clicks his own seatbelt in place before he backs out of the place, driving first on familiar roads until it led to unfamiliar roads. Empty roads.

No cars were in sight.

A normal person may scream and shout. But he wasn't normal and I knew protesting now when the car was on the road wasn't going to get me anywhere.

So I leaned my head against the window and allowed myself to not care for the while. Just a little bit, I tell myself. Just for now, I can thinking about nothing. I will worry about it all later.

All later.

Chapter 8 - Kaya

N ew Chapter!!!

Just a little heads up, this chapter is slightly on the longer side so like usual, I recommend reading it when you have a little more extra time on your hands.

Enjoy reading!!!

"You walked into my life like you had always lived there, like my heart was a home built just for you."

- A. R. Asher

"Kaya, wake up." A voice softly calls out as a click sound registers in my ears. I didn't want to move or wake up. It was so warm, so comfortable, so nice.

Wait. No. Hold on a second. I slept? In peace?

I jerk upright and find that the car had stopped moving, my seatbelt no longer in place, a large towel thrown over me and him hovering above me. His head was cocked to the side, observing me like a hawk would it's prey.

"Where are we?" I ask as I look around the place. Nothing felt remotely familiar, and I wasn't sure whether I should be relieved that I wasn't close to home or if I should feel anxious because I didn't know where I was.

"Get out." was the only reply I get as he backs away to give me the space to get out of his car.

Wherever this place was, it was far away from the cemetery and his and my house. Surprisingly, my clothes were almost dry, and my hair was now only just a little damp.

As I get out of the car, I try to look around again. It had stopped raining, but the skies remained grey and cloudy, still threatening for more rainfall and thunder. Around us, there were nothing but trees and bushes. No sounds of traffic, or people could be heard. It was complete silence. But not the awkward or uncomfortable kind. The silence was peaceful. If only my mind was this quiet.

He closes the car door behind me and locks the car before turning around and starts walking off. Like the lost puppy I was, I obediently follow, not wanting to be left behind in the middle of nowhere. Sometimes I wished to be like his sister Minori just so I can live independently and tackle down any man or woman. But the thought of killing in cold blood will never be something I would be capable of.

It doesn't take long for the uneven rock filled gravel to turn into smooth concrete that leads to large glossy black gates that situates itself in front of a . . . mansion? Here in the middle of nowhere?

He taps in some code and the gate immediately opens and I watch in awe. I grew up surrounded by wealth and everything that screams money, but I was yet to see a mansion that looked as beautiful as this. So modern yet so vintage?

It was styled in a bold yet subtle wooden tree house way, but each pillar and modelling of the house was framed in black emitting an elegant finish to the mansion. Most walls from I could see were made of glass which enabled access to the calming view of rows after rows of trees and nature. At the top of mansion, I could see railing which made me believing that maybe you could even watch the view in something similar to that of a bird's eye view. Perfect for star gazing I think to myself.

"What are you doing? Come." He demands in that authoritative way that for reasons unknown to me loved and hated at the same time. I oblige, quickly walk past the gates and inside the mansion door.

He once again punches in some code that opened the door to the mansion, which made me wonder if the two were the same. But I immediately shake the thought remembering who this man was. No way even in death would he have use the same code.

He leads me inside and I unconsciously whisper out, "wow."

This place would be any person's dream home.

Home. It felt like home. The interior of this place was very similar to that of the exterior with wood finishing floors, tables, and chairs, paired with black metal stairs, and a few minor details like the rugs on the floor, cushions on the sofa and lighting brought this place together.

It was so warm, cozy, welcoming.

No, that sounds extremely strange. That man is the opposite of all of that.

"Why did you bring me here?" I interrogate, wrapping my arms around my torso. I was a little too late to realise that my words were contradicting my actions. I immediately unwrap them.

Anyhow, I can't understand why he would take me to such place like this.

"Because you probably wouldn't have gone home tonight. Figured it'd be best if I monitored you from here." He replies as he begins to strip off his suit jacket and neatly hangs it on the coat hanger.

A normal person should find it unsettling that someone could somehow read your thoughts, but it was him we were talking about. Of course he would know that I probably would have stayed under the rain until my mind was clear enough to go back home.

"Go take a shower. You were shivering like stray cat who didn't have food in days. The bathroom is the last door down the corridor."

The comment was unnecessary, but the thought of a hot shower sounded a little too good and so I shamelessly walked down the wood tiled corridor without even making a remark back.

Opening the door that led to the bathroom, which was also simple and elegant in design, I peel off all my clothes and hop into the scalding shower, just the way I like it.

I still had no idea where I was, or what his real intention of keeping me here was but I allowed myself to just enjoy this amazingly warm shower in peace. I can think about all those complicating things a little later.

However like all things that starts with a little moment of peace, it gets pulled away from your grasp. This one in the shape and form of him coming into the bathroom while I was still showering. Still showering! Yes, the hot water produced steam, fogging up the shower glass but that didn't cover everything!

"What the hell Ryo! Get out!" I scream, turning around, facing the wall.

"There's nothing there that I haven't seen Kaya. I'm just bringing you spare clothes." He talks back, voice unaffected while placing a pile of clothes on the space next to the sink before leaving and shutting the door. Yeah, I may or may not have peaked over my shoulder.

Sure he may have seen everything I own but that didn't mean he was granted the access to see it like it was nothing. But I suppose to him it was nothing. All just body parts with its functional anatomy. Parts he could use to end one's life.

I end the shower, more annoyed than I was before coming into this place and dry myself with a usually soft towel that I was contemplating on whether I should bring back home and pick up the clothes that he brought over.

I don't know why I was surprised but they were his clothes. I've seen him wearing these before and it smelt just like him. Don't ask if I inhaled deeply or not. I didn't . . .

Pretending to not think much of it, I slip them on and walk out of the bathroom and down the corridor. Maybe it was because I adopted the habit of looking down instead of up or just because of my careless nature my mother always likes to point out but I come crashing against something that wasn't quite a wall.

"Do you make it a habit of yours to bump into people now?" He questions as he messily dry his hair with a towel, only wearing pants, his abs flex with each back and forth movement from drying his hair and his irezumi tattoos that decorates the upper half of his body were on full display.

I still vividly remember when he got his first one. It was when he was 14 years old, on his left arm, dragon scales that wrapped around it. You would expect people to show off their tattoos, but he never did. I wasn't quite sure what he thought of it, but his tattoo collection continued to grow in numbers. I hadn't see the full picture in over nine years and there were more added to the collection. The crane which I knew definitely symbolised his sister, the countless Sakura's representing his organization and chrysanthemum that decorated his left chest. I wasn't too sure what they symbolise, but it was a common irezumi choice in our world.

"I'll be more careful." I reply looking away from him.

He takes in a sharp inhale before he grips my chin between his fingers, forcing me to look up at him once again. I look at his clean face, large deep brown eyes that appear almost black, and his ruffled pitch-black hair that was now covering his forehead which is usually on display for that clean look. And inhale his scent. That minty, lavender, lemon scent. Clean and fresh. Deceptive and subtle.

"What did I say about looking away from me?" He interrogates in that deceivingly calm demeanour. But this was the thing, when he talks in that manner, that authoritative manner, you had no choice but to comply. To obey and follow.

"To not do it." I answer.

"Exactly. So why did you do it?"

"I-I. . ." I stutter out, diverting my eyes.

"Eyes on me Kaya." He demands, his eyes firmly on mine.

"I'm t-tired." Stammering, I answering a little too emotionally. These fuck-ing emotions taking control of every part of my mind and body.

I didn't know what I was expecting but his gaze softening wasn't one of them. Slowly, his fingers pull away from my chin and a stupid part of me mourned the loss of warmth and touch from him.

"There are plenty of rooms down the corridor. Choose any and go sleep." He says as his hands slowly gets put away into the pocket of his pants.

"Thanks," I say before turning around to retreat to one of the rooms.

No, why was I going to sleep in a place I don't even know?

But I slept peacefully in the car. How long has it been since I've been able to sleep without reliving that time?

Surely I can have another sleep without it being riddled with nightmares I think to myself before like on cue, I yawn and collapse onto the bed. Letting the sleepiness in my system take control, I drift off to yet another sleep of the day.

Chapter 9 - Ryosuke

N ew Chapter!!!

Happy Reading□□

"Not everything in the heart can be said,

so God created sighs, tears, long sleep, cold smiles and shivering hands."

- Nizar Quabbani

The human mind is a complicated thing. Feelings are a complicated thing.

Kaya pretends to be mean so that her sister, Hikari would hate her. Hikari does the exact same thing for reasons I could only imagine where similar or the same.

But when I receive a call from Hikari that Kaya had left her house to presumably go to Kenji's grave, I was already out the door.

Kaya may go over to the graveyeard more often than any other person I knew but the reasons why she went were quite limited.

One, she missed him.

Two, she goes asking if she could go over to him.

Today, the reason was number two, and I hated it.

I wanted nothing more than to crush those thoughts away into specks that can't even be seen under the standard microscope. Scratch that, I want to crush those thoughts away into absolute nothingness and I was certain Kenji would think the same. He protected and sacrificed his life so that she would live and I sure as hell will make sure she does just that. Live.

Twirling my sake cup, I continue to observe the dreary weather and endless scenery of just trees. I wasn't quite sure what prompted me to purchase this plot of land and build this mansion. Hidden away from normal society and our world. Filled with the only sounds of nature, the wind, the rustling of leaves, the birds and the like.

Looking or hearing those kinds of things don't usually calm me like most people do but for some reason, I liked it. The peace, the quiet, the emptiness of it all. It felt right. Especially with her in it.

"No! Move! No!" Her voice screams out in agony from the opposite end of the building. Her words echoes against the walls in a way I knew all too well. The trapped feeling, the cries that go unheard, the scenarios and realities that'll never change regardless of how hard you try to modify it to create a new ending.

I make my way over to where she slept and open the door, finding her tangled between the sheets, her breathing ragged, sweat beading against her forehead, tears spilling from her lids every now and then as she continues to mouth out the following.

"Move. . . Kenji you need to move . . . no . . . no . . . move . . . no. . . don't leave me. . . no. . . "

I wasn't new to witnessing nightmares. Nightmares that are often so severe sometimes you avoid the idea of sleeping altogether. Minori used to do that and sometimes popped sleeping pills like candy which can often worsen her mood and overall health.

Normally I would wake up the person. They were usually subjected to these nightmares most nights and it would be better to end it for them, forcefully.

But it had been a while since I have seen her in this state. I would have imagined it would have improved or at least the duration in which she suffers would be shortened. That was the case with most people including Minori. She still sees them from time to time, but it has lessened significantly.

However, it seems that wasn't the case for her.

"Please . . . p-please don't . . . leave me . . . No! No! . . . I'm sorry. . . I-I'm so, so sorry. . . no . . .s-sorry . . . I should have . . . I should . . ."

I didn't want to hear the rest anymore.

I take seat on the edge of the bed and firmly hold onto her arms. People tend to thrash and hurt themselves when they wake up from nightmares. Or at least Minori did.

"Kaya, wake up," I shake her as another stimulant to wake her. But it only seems to worsen her state, her whole face scrunches, and she once again, begins to scream. I didn't really ever mind her screaming at me but her screaming because she was suffering wasn't something I wanted to hear.

"Kaya, wake up," I repeat and it does the job. Or at least physically.

Her eyes open wide, and she was seeing something that wasn't me. Her breath gets hitched in her throat and her whole body stiffens in my hold.

"I . . . I'm sorry Mom," she sobs. "I'm so sorry. I was wrong. I should've died. I-I'm so sorry."

It takes everything within me not to react. I can't even get rid of her mother because the girl in front of me would suffer even further. I can't even understand how her mother was even capable of making her feel this way, my mother would never dare.

Taking a deep breath to calm myself, I call out to her. "Kaya, it's me. Ryo."

"Ryo?" She whispers, her face contorting into that of a mixture of relief and pain.

"Yes," I slide my arm underneath her shoulders and back and bring her up into a sitting position so I could see her face more clearly. Her eyes were red, and her eyelids were a little swollen, her cheeks were flushed, and her hair was tangled and sticky from the thrashing and tears.

"Do you want me to bring you water?"

She shakes her head.

"Do you want to take a shower?"

She shakes her head again.

"What would you like to do?"

She looks away from me which I hated more than I should, but she leans in closer and lightly rests her head against my chest and just stays there.

Minori did that often too. She never explained to me why she did it or why it made her feel calm, but I assumed it brings them a sense of safety. Or the feeling that they aren't alone. Either way, I didn't mind the action, it wasn't uncomfortable, nor did it feel odd in any way so if that makes them feel better I just let them stay there.

Using my fingers, I gently comb through her hair while my other arm wraps around her body, bringing her closer to me. If physical barrier was what she needed, I could give that to her.

It doesn't take long for her breathing to even out, drifting back into sleep and for me to scoop her up into my arms and leave the room to opt for another room to sleep in. It would be better to sleep in clean sheets anyway.

I tuck her in and begin to peel myself off from her, but then, she grabs my finger. I have no idea if this was just instinct or some odd reflex thing that I lacked knowledge in but something within me urged me to stay by her side.

Like I should stay with her.

So I did.

Chapter 10 - Kaya

- -

N ew Chapter!!!

These few chapters have been relatively peaceful and ngl I kind of enjoy writing these mundane scenes. The peace before the conflict if you will.

Anyways, happy reading!!!

"A lot of people struggle with sleep because sleep requires peace."

- Unknown

Waking up from the morning sun beaming down at my face with its glare, the scent of strong coffee drifts into my nose, awakening my need for caffeine. But that wasn't what was on the forefront of my mind.

It happened again.

The no nightmare thing. When he was around.

Well, I did have one before that, but he wasn't next to me. Maybe it was because my subconscious associated him with safety or protection, which was ridiculous but the two times I was aware that he was next to me were the two times my sleep wasn't riddled with a replay of the past.

Heat rises to my cheeks and a smile forms on my face, but it quickly slips when I remember the embarrassing act I did for him to stay with me. I smack my face into the palms of my hands.

I wasn't asleep when he moved me from the room I slept in prior to the one I was in right now. I wasn't asleep when he tucked me in the sheets. And I wasn't asleep when I grabbed his finger.

It might've been a cowards move and slightly embarrassing, okay extremely embarrassing, if he knew I was pretending to be asleep, but I didn't have it within me to regret my choice of action.

His minty, clean scent still lingered in the sheets and on me from his clothes, resulting in a familiar comforting feel washing over me and I allow myself to take a deep inhale. He probably didn't actually sleep with me because his sleep schedule was worse than mine, but he stayed. He stayed with me and that was all I needed, and I was just thankful that he entertained the idea.

Peeling the comforter off me, I make my way out of the room and towards where the coffee scent lingered stronger in the air.

And then obviously, I see him. He was already dressed perfectly with a crips white dress shirt, his hair styled in that perfect ratio that made it look clean and perfect. Without eyeing the coffee in his right hand, he scrolls through whatever it was he was looking at before taking a graciously elegant sip of that coffee.

This was the thing with the Sakurazuki's, their way of eating and drinking like nobility. Hell it could even be like royalty. Effortless, clean, and elegant. They genuinely made us appear like peasants with no table manners when you eat with them. Sorry, dine with them.

He doesn't even spare me a glance when he greets me with a "sit down," placing his cup and phone down, graciously getting out of his chair to walk over towards the kitchen behind the dinning area.

I obediently sit down on an empty seat opposite to where he was sitting, shamelessly watching him do the things he does in the kitchen.

You couldn't convince me otherwise, men in the kitchen are good looking.

I continue watching him as he swiftly places two bowl of rice, miso soup and grilled fish onto its respective trays before he brings them over. One for me and one for him.

I don't remember when it was the last time I had breakfast with him. Was it when we were twelve or thirteen years old when me and Kaito came over for a sleep over? That was actually our parents getting together and planning some things I can't remember now but it was fun for us kids while the adults pondered and wondered about their next move. Well he may not have, but I did. Anyhow, point was, it was a little awkward having a breakfast with him on a random Wednesday in the middle of who knows where at 25 years old, looking like your typical dirt-poor Cinderella. Overworked, undervalued and a laughingstock.

I shook the thought away, choosing to admire my breakfast.

The breakfast was a simple, traditional Japanese breakfast. I didn't even eat breakfast these days. The thought just seemed like a waste of time, like sleep, I could live without having breakfast every morning. But even with its simplicity, the food looked delicious and nostalgic. If only time machine existed.

"I didn't know you were able to cook," I muse as I watch him settle into his chair like a King would to his throne. "Did Ane-san teach you how to cook? Or did you ask one of the kitchen staff to teach you?" I probe even though I already knew the answer.

His mother, who we call Ane-san in our organization as a term for older sister, was a sweet woman with a heart made of steel. She was also my second mother. More like your only mother. Damn me and these thoughts.

Unlike the Oyabun, his father, who taught him everything through raw experience – both good and bad, Anee-san taught him through experiences that'll last him a lifetime.

"Mum." He replies, confirming the answer I had in mind.

I begin to eat the food, remembering to mutter 'itadakimasu', a phrase that basically thanked those who made the food in Japanese. It was a little weird saying the word that I haven't said in so long, but it also felt right.

The meals goes through in comfortable silence, with me nodding every now and then as I eat the rice because I never realised how Japanese or Asian I was until I have eaten this bowl of rice.

"Weather's nice today. We'll learn to shoot." He says out of the blue and I nod along, still thoroughly enjoying my meal.

Wait, hold up. Shoot? Learn to shoot?

"Wait, go back. What did you say?"

"You'll learn to shoot. I can't leave you vulnerable when situations turn unfavourable." He explains like it was a no brainer before sipping on another cup of coffee. Since when did he get a new full cup?

"So I can have a gun?" I question. Not the most important question and he would probably flip the meaning behind this but oh well.

"No. The only situation you'll be handed a gun is when I can predict situations will go south or when the situation has already turned south. Although the latter is highly unlikely."

"Oh okay."

"Your clothes are in the dryer. Meet me outside." And then he take his own tray with empty bowls and plates along with mine before he goes back into the kitchen, rolling his sleeves to begin washing the dishes.

You would think for a wealthy man who had maids and helpers wouldn't have a clue how to wash dishes but like with the cooking, I assume Ane-san taught him these things too.

Maybe I should have offered to wash instead but I don't like washing and he did indirectly tell me to get ready. . .

So, I made my way to laundry room located downstairs, where there was an unnecessarily large washing machine, a dryer and even space to iron and fold clothes.

The idea of getting out of the clothes I was currently in was for some reason made me hesitant, but such thought was quite stupid on its own, so I chase the thought away and slip into my wide jeans and plain white top.

I breathe in and only smell my body wash, plain and boring. It brought normalcy but nothing more.

And for some reason, that unsettled me most.

Chapter 11 - Ryosuke

Ｎew Chapter

Warning: Gun/weaponry are mentioned within this chapter. Please take care of yourselves and read what is most comfortable for you.

The real deal is now about to start from now hehehe. Very excited for the next few chapters.

Enjoy reading!!!□

"It"s so much darker when a light goes out

than it would have been if it had never shone."

- John Steinbeck

I had no idea what prompted me to make her learn how to use a gun.

She didn't need to know or learn how to use one. I would never take her with me anywhere that would warrant a need to use a gun.

I could lie to myself and say that regardless of me being by her side, she could still be in danger, that she'll be vulnerable, an obvious target. But the naked truth was, I just needed her close to me.

I don't sleep.

Not for the same reason as Minori or Kaya. I just can't sleep. Sleep never came naturally to me like majority of the population and in the small handful of hours I do get sleep, it's restless and hardly rejuvenating.

When I decided to lay next to her last night, I imagined it would go along the same way I kept Minori company when she slept after a nightmare. Give her a sense of protection, a barrier, a guard. Let her feel safe enough to be able to sleep. But it seems she was the one who brought me the calm.

After a couple of minutes of observing her as she slept, brushing through her tangled hair with my fingers, I watched as her cheeks slowly retrieved back its healthy punk hue. I traced with my eyes her full pink lips that were slightly open apart and those thick long lashes fluttering before unknowingly, closed my eyes and slept too.

It was rejuvenating as it was calming. And it was one of the most peaceful moments I have experienced in a long time.

And thankfully, she hadn't experienced any nightmares thereafter.

Making myself busy with setting up the target and check that I do in fact have a loaded gun with me, I start walking several feet back, the grassy ground slightly soft from the morning dew under my leather shoes.

Out of the corner of my eye, she reappears in her own clothes with her long black hair tied back walking over towards me. Kaya often commented that she was jealous of the way Minori walks elegantly commanding respect, but I couldn't understand her envy. Sure, my sister yielded power that demanded respect, but Kaya walked in a way that brought everyone's attention on her. It wasn't demanding or commanding. It was natural and effortless.

"Are we going to stand here all day?" She questioned sarcastically, crossing her arms as she glared up at my face.

I smile to myself. That was more like it.

"I'm sure you like the idea of doing nothing all day," I drawled handing her the weapon. "But no, we are not going to stand here all day."

She takes the gun with two hands, holding it away from her, not knowing what to do with it. I stand behind her, reaching my arm over hers, placing her fingers where it should be, ensuring her grip was strong but loose enough for easier movement. She stays silent throughout the process, letting me do the work, her eyes tracking what needed to be done.

Kaya has always been a fast learner. She loathes the idea of losing or not being able to do things. It didn't matter whether that be academics, sports, public speaking, or petty games; she had to be the number one. But that quality of hers assured me that she would be able to learn how to shoot in an hour or two, if not less.

"Stand shoulder width apart." I command, waiting for her to follow. "Arms straight ahead and loose. But not weak." I check that her arms are lose enough for the minor impact. "Finger on the trigger and look straight ahead at your target. Never, look away from your target."

She takes in a sharp inhale to settle herself, as she aligns the gun with her target.

"Pull the trigger when you're ready."

She takes her time to prepare herself, breathing in deeply, exhaling just as deep. But once ready, she pulls on the trigger, her body jerking slightly

I was even more impressed. She was taking this session more seriously than I'd initially thought. But then again, she wasn't the same Kaya I grew up with. This Kaya was darker, , and most annoyingly, cautious.

Chaotic Kaya was far more interesting.

"Right here," I point to her knee, "or here," using my finger on my other hand, I point at her mid-thigh. "Or anywhere that has a load of nerves that can feel pain more sensitively."

"Like the genitals?"

"Yes."

"What about your shins? There isn't much muscle or fat protecting it. Would it hurt?"

"Yes."

"If I aim for the arteries would that make them bleed to death?"

"Depends on if they're mobile enough to get away and seek medical attention."

"If I aim for the arteries after shooting their knees and feet," she pauses, thinking, "and their arms, will they die of blood loss?"

"Most likely," I say flatly to mask the fact that I was thoroughly entertained by her stubbornness. "Go again. One shot doesn't determine your talent." I taunted her, just for good measure as I return to my position behind her. Whatever fight she had in her right now, I needed more of it.

She huffs out in annoyance, rolling her eyes before making sure to glare at me as she straightens her body, loosening her arms, and carefully aims for the target ahead.

backwards towards my front as the bullet suspends into the air and lodges itself on the target not too far off the centre.

"Not bad." I comment quite satisfied.

"Where am I supposed to shoot on people?" She asked still in position, facing away from me.

I'm not going to lie; I liked her question. These were the times I knew she wasn't raised like normal girl or woman. She thought like one of us. We didn't have the luxury to think that our lives would be forever peaceful or protected. Not matter how much power or money you had; we were constantly in front of death's door.

One minute you could be alive. The next? Eyes open, body cold, and bullet wedged between said open eye.

Moving in front of her, I raise my arms, my thumb above my fist, my index finger extended, pointing towards the tip of her nose, "here."

"The brainstem," she murmurs, understanding the reason why without explanation.

Mirroring my movement, she points her finger to my nose, and stares intently, memorising the spot. She could also be analysing how she could shoot there and from what distance would be most effective. If there was one thing we had in common, we both went ahead to figure out all the moves required to make the one move. Life was like shougi, Japanese chess. If you calculate accurately, move the pieces where it was the most effective while considering all the angles your opponent will take, you were set to win.

Keeping her finger on me, she asks, "Where should I shoot if I want them to suffer?"

attention on her. It wasn't demanding or commanding. It was natural and effortless.

"Are we going to stand here all day?" She questioned sarcastically, crossing her arms as she glared up at my face.

I smile to myself. That was more like it.

"I'm sure you like the idea of doing nothing all day," I drawled handing her the weapon. "But no, we are not going to stand here all day."

She takes the gun with two hands, holding it away from her, not knowing what to do with it. I stand behind her, reaching my arm over hers, placing her fingers where it should be, ensuring her grip was strong but loose enough for easier movement. She stays silent throughout the process, letting me do the work, her eyes tracking what needed to be done.

Kaya has always been a fast learner. She loathes the idea of losing or not being able to do things. It didn't matter whether that be academics, sports, public speaking, or petty games; she had to be the number one. But that quality of hers assured me that she would be able to learn how to shoot in an hour or two, if not less.

"Stand shoulder width apart." I command, waiting for her to follow. "Arms straight ahead and loose. But not weak." I check that her arms are lose enough for the minor impact. "Finger on the trigger and look straight ahead at your target. Never, look away from your target."

She takes in a sharp inhale to settle herself, as she aligns the gun with her target.

"Pull the trigger when you're ready."

She takes her time to prepare herself, breathing in deeply, exhaling just as deep. But once ready, she pulls on the trigger, her body jerking slightly

I could lie to myself and say that regardless of me being by her side, she could still be in danger, that she'll be vulnerable, an obvious target. But the naked truth was, I just needed her close to me.

I don't sleep.

Not for the same reason as Minori or Kaya. I just can't sleep. Sleep never came naturally to me like majority of the population and in the small handful of hours I do get sleep, it's restless and hardly rejuvenating.

When I decided to lay next to her last night, I imagined it would go along the same way I kept Minori company when she slept after a nightmare. Give her a sense of protection, a barrier, a guard. Let her feel safe enough to be able to sleep. But it seems she was the one who brought me the calm.

After a couple of minutes of observing her as she slept, brushing through her tangled hair with my fingers, I watched as her cheeks slowly retrieved back its healthy punk hue. I traced with my eyes her full pink lips that were slightly open apart and those thick long lashes fluttering before unknowingly, closed my eyes and slept too.

It was rejuvenating as it was calming. And it was one of the most peaceful moments I have experienced in a long time.

And thankfully, she hadn't experienced any nightmares thereafter.

Making myself busy with setting up the target and check that I do in fact have a loaded gun with me, I start walking several feet back, the grassy ground slightly soft from the morning dew under my leather shoes.

Out of the corner of my eye, she reappears in her own clothes with her long black hair tied back walking over towards me. Kaya often commented that she was jealous of the way Minori walks elegantly commanding respect, but I couldn't understand her envy. Sure, my sister yielded power that demanded respect, but Kaya walked in a way that brought everyone's

She shoots, hitting the target directly at its centre. Bulls eye. Not bad. Not bad at all. But clearly, she had a point to prove and two bullets wasn't enough and that headstrong mindset of hers made her shoot the remaining 4 bullets one after another. All within the centre target.

If she were this good, I should've let her hold a gun sooner. Minori was an excellent sniper but not a skilled shooter. Shooting wasn't my choice when ending one's life since I preferred to get messy and personal, but it was a skill necessary for survival.

But now I realise I found talent in someone who was always close but far to me, both at the same time.

"You were saying?" She mimics my flat tone, turning her head to the side, those light brown eyes like earth stones still glaring at me.

"You have talent."

"What?" She questions like she couldn't comprehend the words that I just said.

"You have talent." I repeat talking the gun from her hand. It was empty so it was good as useless but if Kaya where anything to go by, she constantly made nothing into something.

"What happened to you?" She grimaces her face like she was seeing an alien within me.

"I could ask the same question."

That shuts her up and although that was my intention, I soon realise I prefer her talking. I prefer hearing her voice. I prefer her engaging with me.

"Having a sister and a mother like mine teaches you that you need to offer acknowledgment where it's due." I say answering her rhetorical question while placing the weapon back into the holster. "And I only said you have talent. That is a fact. I don't like lies, let alone uttering them."

"Glad to know you're still the same person from ten years ago," she muttered before rolling her eyes. But despite her obvious distaste in my answer, a small smile appears on her face. The two contradicting emotions confused me and yet I knew what I felt. I felt content, good.

My phone rings and vibrates inside my pockets. I take out, finding Kaito's name. For him to call me when I told him not to bother me must mean he has a good enough reason to interrupt me. I answer.

"What is it?" I asked annoyed, facing away from her.

"Are you still with Kaya?" Kaito asked, his usually cheerful tone abandoned and replaced with a flat one.

"Yeah."

"Her mother's condition deteriorated and was rushed to hospital."

This wasn't unexpected but did it have to be now? When for the first time in a long time, she smiled naturally?

Tapping my finger on the phone, I close my eyes weighing the options.

"Ryo?" He called out from the line, asking for my answer.

"We'll be there." I replied after a short while before cutting off the call.

"Is everything alright?" Kaya questioned, appearing right in front of me in the time I had my eyes closed. "Did something happen?"

Genuine concerned etched onto her face, the small but mischievous smile wiped away. And I knew I wouldn't see them for a while. She was going to be consumed with a surge of emotions that'll drown and asphyxiate her. She was going to become more reckless.

And she was going to suffer.

As though her life were written in ink purely created for suffering and misery.

For torment and anguish.

For . . . pain.

Chapter 12 - Kaya

N ew Chapter

Warning: Health deterioration, grief, loss, verbal abuse and negative self-talk is explored within this chapter. Please read what is comfortable for you.

This chapter is quite heavy in theme and quite lengthy. Please do read the warning before reading through.

Enjoy your reading time.

"Then suddenly you're left all alone with your body that can't love you and your will that can't save you."

- Rainer Maria Rilke

Deterioration. A process in which something or someone is becoming worse in state.

My mother was deteriorating.

A whole whirlwind of emotions and feelings were crashing into my already damaged mind, feeling everything and nothing at all both at once, confusing me all the more. Concern, fear, distress and disgustingly, relief. Relief knowing she was going to die. Relief in knowing I would no longer be responsible for her. Relief in knowing I was one step closer to letting myself free and finish this miserable life.

"Stop doing that," he demanded in that reassured manner, putting me off guard. Suddenly being inside the car felt claustrophobic despite the spacious design.

"Huh?" I turn my attention to him as he drove with nonchalance I wished to possess.

"Stop biting on your mouth."

Tasting the familiar copper taste, I realise I was biting on my mouth the whole ride. I instantly feel conscious and wipe my mouth to get rid of any blood staining my lips before gritting my teeth to prevent biting again.

Not knowing the roads was an uncomfortable thing. I didn't know where we were or how long it'll take to get back home. And I still couldn't decide whether I wanted this drive back home to be a quick one to get to my mother or want it to be the longest drive possible just to delay the inevitable.

I was always indecisive by nature but right now, it really wasn't helping.

"Drink." He held a thermos bottle right in front of my face while continuing to skilfully, steering the wheel. The ability he had to just erase his presence only to appear in front of you still takes me by surprise. I take the bottle almost begrudgingly but take a sip of the contents inside.

Chamomile tea.

As demanding as he was, he prepared this for me.

And this was the thing; he knew me more than I knew myself.

"Thanks, for the tea."

He gives an affirmative sound and continued to concentrate on the roads ahead. Me on the other hand, continued to sip the tea, knowing well that the calming effects only happen if you drank it consistently but regardless, I felt the desired effect as I watched the scenery pass by.

Children played on playgrounds gleefully as some mothers chattered amongst each other or chased their own child. Men and women in smart formal wear had their phones pressed to their ear as they argued with whoever was on the other side of the line. Elderly couples gave each other loving glances as they take a stroll.

So many different people at different points in life, but so content with what they have and own. At least on the outside. At least from what I could see exteriorly.

"I know you probably won't answer," I began, placing the thermos down as I continued to watch the view, "but if you could be anything you want to be in your next life, who or what would you want to be?"

A couple beats of silence passes, and I was almost certain he wasn't going to answer like I predicted.

"Myself."He replied. I wait for several moments, expecting an explanation that never came.

Why am I not even surprised? Of course this asshole, who's so sure of himself would want to reborn into himself again. I fear for the planet we call home. I rolled my eyes.

"What do you want to be?" He questioned back, surprising me that he cared to entertain me.

"Me?"

"Yes you."

Despite all the many times I have thought of this question, I still had to think for a little while to give an answer.

"I want to be anything but living breathing things. I want to be abiotic." I finally answered.

"Not possible."

"I didn't say it had to be possible. You could become a fire breathing dragon for all I care."

"So you want to be water or soil or something just as monotonous?"

"What's so bad about that?" I retorted, crossing my arms.

"You can find that answer yourself. Besides, we're here."

The car came to a stop, just outside the hospital building and the panic that surprisingly was absent for a little while, decided to show it's ugly face. My body trembled with uncertainty and my mind began to cloud with all the possible scenarios.

My mother tied to machines. My mother intubated. My mother dead.

"Kaya, it will be fine."

I look to my side, finding that the door was already open for me and instead of being in the driver's seat, he was next to me, holding out his hand. His arms with his intricate tattoos were now covered by his shirt in an attempt to blend with society but there was no denying that those arms were strong and powerful. But his hands? They were large and yet, so welcoming. Another quality that could be the furthest thing from the person that I knew. The person our organization knew.

The heir. The murderer. The crazy one.

Regardless, I take his hand, climbing out of the car as we both made our way up the elevators, down the abnormally white corridors, with the clogging smell of antiseptic and the unusually bright lights.

I follow his lead like I always had, keeping my eyes on the floor and nowhere else. I wiled myself to breathe in through my nose and out through my mouth.

It was fine. No one's dead. I am not going to find a dead body.

We come to halt somewhere, and the rolling sound of sliding doors registers in my ear. Slowly raising my head, I find Ryosuke blocking whatever lay in the dark room that supposedly led to my mother, waiting for me to enter.

My feet oddly felt heavy but running back now stupid. What kind of idiot is scared of entering a stupid hospital room?

I walk inside.

I find my sister before anything else. Her head resting on the side of the hospital bed where I knew my mother lay. Hikari doesn't move or react as we enter. The rise and fall of her body was the only indication that she was alive.

Guilt grips onto every limb and tightens its hold on my throat.

I let my sister suffer alone with a deteriorating mother, alone. And in all that time, I was having a good time. For a little while, I forgot reality.

How could I ever call myself the older sister?

I was irresponsible. I was selfish, self-absorbing, so fucking self-centred.

And that's why Kenji died. He died because you're good for nothing. You killed him.

"You killed him!" My mother wailed, crumbling against me. My mother who had always prided herself in how she looked was shrivelled up in appearance, her dark brown hair unkempt, her clothes wrinkled and stained with tears.

My father ignored my presence altogether, only blankly staring at my brother's dead body that was only covered by a white sheet cloth.

"You should've died!" My mother screamed in my face, hitting my leg, "I don't need you! I need Kenji!" She grips both of my arms that lay limply on the side of my wheelchair, "You should've never been born."

"That's enough." My father said, pulling my mother to his side. He looks down at me briefly, but nothing that could be described as emotions passed his eyes.

No grief. No disappointment. No hatred.

Just nothing.

And for some reason that hurt more than my mother's words.

Pulling my mother who had long lost her sense of herself through the doors, they both left me in the darkly lit room. Left with me, with my brother. My dead brother. The brother I killed.

I wheeled myself closer to him, telling myself that I had to see him one last time.

My hands mindlessly reached for his face, expecting it to be warm. Expecting it to respond to my touch.

But it was cold, so uncharacteristically cold. Kenji was always warm. Kenji was always bright.

And it didn't respond. His eyes stayed closed. His mouth didn't turn upwards into a smile. His face didn't light up or turn red like it always had when he cracked a joke or saw the girl he was infatuated with.

I grip his hand, his arm, forcing my body out of the stupid wheelchair, only for me to collapse onto the cold floor, the reality dawning down on me. The force of it all pressed down on me as I struggled to get out of the room, the corridors, this god damn white building hell.

I needed to get out of here.

"The doctors said she's stable now. Kaito will drop Hikari-chan off when she wakes up. What do you want to do? Kaya? Kaya!?"

"Get me out of here." I managed to strangle out, shutting my eyes.

"Okay."

I didn't know where I was going, or how my legs moved, but I trusted the arms that wrapped around my body guiding me out of that suffocating room. I feel my body losing any sense of strength and I feel the arms gripping me tighter before it lets go and I sank down onto the ugly hospital lounge couches.

"It's okay. Deep breaths." His hand pulls my head down onto his shoulder while another glides up and down my back almost soothingly.

Emotions familiar and foreign, aggressively attacked me and I didn't know which one to cling on to. I didn't know how I should be acting, and I didn't know what I should be doing.

"Let it out. Let it all out. You'll feel better that way." The soothing hands continue to glide, gently, slowly, tenderly, up and down my back. Over and over again.

I couldn't hear or see much at all, but those words repeated itself in my head, grounding me a little.

"I-It . . . it hurts." I mumble against his shirt.

"That's okay."

"I . . . I d-don't know what to do."

"You don't need to do anything if you don't want to. I'll sort it out."

"Every . . . everyone's leaving m-me."

"I'm not leaving you."

"But y-you did."

" . . . I did. But I will show you now, that I won't."

I didn't trust those words.

But I wanted to.

So desperately.

Because only he would view things objectively stay on my side. Because he was the only person who listened and told me I wasn't wrong.

But the past couldn't be erased. And I was still clinging onto the past, breathing it, living in it.

I couldn't move forward like people told me to. I couldn't forget like people wanted me to.

I was left behind, with people and time marching forward into the future. Living and making a life for themselves, while my legs were stuck in the quicksand, slowly, gradually, swallowing me whole.

Only darkness greeted me.

And stupidly, I always turned to it.

Chapter 13 - Ryosuke

Now Chapter!!!

Just a heads up, this chapter is fairly long so like always, I recommend reading it when you have more time on your hands. If you could read till the end, it is much appreciated.□

Are you enjoying the story so far? I hope you are.

Just some Translations you might need

Onigiri - Triangular Japanese Rice balls

Ane-san - Yakuza boss' (Oyabun's) wife. The word translates older sister.

Washitsu - Traditional Japanese room characterized by tatami floors/mats and fusuma doors

Fusuma - Traditional Japanese sliding doors

H   a   p   p   y
r   e   a   d   i   n   g   .

"Know all the theories, master all the techniques, but as you touch a human soul be just just another human soul."

- C.G. Jung

Conscious of who was sleeping on the other side, I turn the doorknob gradually, soundlessly closing the door behind me.

I did expect her to lose her composure, but I couldn't expect how bad it got. She wasn't merely hyperventilating; she wasn't able to function at all. She became unsteady on her feet until she could barely walk at all, while her eyes darted everywhere as though she was seeing something or someone I could not. Her cries were pained and raw until they turned silent. You could only hear the muffled whimpering as the tears continued to flow and her body shook from the tears and wounds that never healed, leaving a trail of darkness in its wake.

And the only thing I could do was hold her tight until she settled.

"Is she alright?" My mother's concerned voice greets me in Japanese with her dark long hair tied back seamlessly indicating to me she either cooking or arranging flowers.

"Yeah. She just passed out from exhaustion." I replied back, taking off my jacket.

"Is that so," she mumbled to herself, her eyes flickering with concern. "When she wakes up, let me know. I made her some Onigiri. I made some for you too, although I'm not sure if it will exist by the time you go down to eat it. You know how much Kaito eats." She quietly laughs to herself, shaking her head.

My mother was an older sister to all in our organization, hence why she holds the tittle of Ane-san. But the title and role she treasured more than an older sister or wife was being a mother and I knew first-hand just how powerful a loving mother is. They didn't fear power, status, money, or death.

The only thing on their mind were their children and their life.

Naturally by extension, Kaito and Kaya became her children as well. And since my mother adored them like her own, my father cared for them too.

"Now," she stands right in front of me, her soft yellow colored kimono brushing my hand as she cups my face in her warm hands. "I feel like I haven't seen your face in months. It's already hard enough that my daughter left the nest."

"She's comes over at the end of every week," I reasoned, visualising Minori running through the corridors to hug our mother, "and besides, I've only been away for five days. Not months." I said, trying and failing to pry her hands off my face.

"I don't see my children enough." She complained as she brushes her fingers though my hair. "But at least I will gain another daughter, right?"

"What?"

"You know very well who and what I am talking about. You even made her stay by your side at all times. How romantic of you."

"Okasan, it's not what you think it is."

"Mhmm, you may have created some logical explanation for yourself like it was for her benefit but here," she points to my chest, "you know very well it was for your benefit."

This was why women, especially this woman, scared me.

"But keep this in mind. That girl there," she nods towards the door behind me, "she's delicate. You can't love her silently. That only grows false hope and doubt in her. You must love her loudly, openly."

"Okasan I don't-"

"I'm not hearing the rest of that nonsense." She scolds placing her hand on top of my mouth. "Go downstairs and entertain your dear friend. And steal back those Onigiri's while you're at it." She smiles, patting my cheeks like I was still four years old in her mind and walks away towards my father's office.

Begrudgingly I make my way downstairs, deleting the conversation from my mind and enter the washitsu room that was made specifically for us to play around. But even after returning back here, we rarely hung out in this room anymore. Sliding the fusuma door open, I find my friend biting into a rice cracker. That only meant he finished all those Onigiri rice balls.

"Is all you do eat in here?"

"Hey, your mother's cooking is ridiculously delicious." Kaito yaps back without missing a beat. "So yes, I will be constantly eating under this roof. She even said that I was her second son." He takes another bite of the round, rice snack. "Who knows maybe I'm her favorite?"

"What update do you have?" I cut the nonsense out, lowering down onto the cushion on the floor.

"You seriously have no clue how to lay back do you?" He grabs another rice cracker and takes a bite loud enough for me to take the bowl with the crackers and put it behind me.

"That's not fair." Pointing at me, he demands me to give the bowl back with his eyes.

"What's not fair is that I can't even have a moment of peace in my own home." I retorted back, making no move to return the item.

"Give it back to me after the report then."

"Fine."

"Okay." He nodded returning to the situation at hand. "So, I asked Hikari about -"

"Since when do you call her by her name alone?" I interrupt. Calling someone's name on its own in Japanese culture only happens when you are close to the person, usually friends, and those the same age as you. Not for parents, not for someone who is older or younger than you.

"Oh, uh, I slipped. Hikari-chan. Whatever, she said Kaya was doing the task you asked her to do. Checked it and this was the result." He hands over the printed paper with Kaya's findings. I take the paper, scanning the words to find the pertinent information.

Haruto Sato allegedly behind the missing 24 thousand dollars. Highly unlikely.

"Should I look into it further?" He asks, peering down.

"No, I'll make Kaya finish the job."

We had plenty of technology enthusiasts to our disposal but if I gave her something to do, her mind would be on the task and not wandering to areas it shouldn't be. It wasn't the most time-effective option, but it had more benefits in the long run.

"Got it. Ah, also Akira has been causing some trouble. The whole group got arrested," he laughs under his breath. "I swear all they like to do is cause trouble but can't blame them," he shrugs. They can't even breathe without being hounded by the government dogs, let alone have fun." The corner of his mouth turns up with what I think was amusement.

Akira and his minions were kids that I foolishly decided to take in a couple of years ago after they caused much nuisance on the roads with their motorcycles back in Japan. Here, their endeavour in wreaking havoc on roads were more achievable without the attention but now I was realising that was no longer the case. I needed to knock some much-needed discipline and dignity into those looseheads sooner rather than later.

"Are they out?" I questioned, exasperated.

"Yeah. Money was all that was needed to get them out. But they're almost of age, won't be as easy after a couple of months."

That training session I was planning for them was going to come into play much sooner than I had arranged for but since I took them in, I was responsible for them and their life.

"They are banned from the roads unless I tell them otherwise. Tell them to meet me in the shed first thing tomorrow at dawn."

"Alright," he closes his eyes and claps his hands together once, "may the heavens bless them."

"May that heavens bless you too. You're joining."

"What?!" His mouth leaves hanging open, as his face slowly twisted in obvious disgust. "I do not need training. I have a fine amount of endurance and strength as well as you and Oyabun's favourite word in mind."

"I don't care if you think you have sufficient amount of endurance or strength and understand the word discipline. I need to see it with my own eyes, so I will see your sorry morning existence at dawn tomorrow."

"Might I give you some advice? You should learn the word kindness and nice. That may come in handy in the -"

"Kindness is derived from Proto-Germanic meaning native or family. Therefore kindness from me is reserved for my mother and sister. The word nice is from Latin meaning foolish or weak so no, I will not be nice. But some advice for you, is to take yourself out of this home to your own home and sleep so can come back here with the most energy you can obtain."

"You are disgustingly nerdy." He throws his arms in the air like a clown. "Why do I even care about your nerdy ass?"

Taking a few crackers for myself I hand him back the bowl filled with the rice crackers which he takes without question and with speed I was expecting to see tomorrow morning.

"I ask a similar question every day." I said, taking a bite of the rice snack.

From behind I hear the door slide open and a soft gasp escape. I could almost feel the panicked rise and fall of her chest and see her soft round face thinking whether she should run back the way she came from.

"Oh, morning princess. Good sleep?" Kaito asked taking a huge bite of another cracker.

"Uh, yeah I guess. Sorry, was I interrupting something?" I could hear her fidgeting with her fingernails - a habit she had ever since I knew her, a nervous tick.

"Nope, His Highness and I just finished with the reports. Is that more Onigiri!?"

"Yeah. Ane-san made more." She walks over before kneeling down between us, placing the tray filled with more rice balls my mother made on the low wooden table. "She said you would want some more and that," she turns to face me with a hint of pink coloring her cheeks, "Ryo probably didn't have any because you ate them all."

"How does she know everything!? Does she have more than two set of eyes?" Kaito scrunches his face before delightfully taking a rice ball.

"Wait, what are you doing?" Kaya questioned swatting my hand.

"You don't have a fever." I retract my hand away from her forehead, thinking of all the other possible reason why she was red in the face.

"I'm warm because I just woke up!" She retorted, placing both of her hands on her forehead where my hands were. Her face only flushed brighter, but I could only focus on those lips, pink and full. I wanted to bite it, suck on it, claim it as mine.

I grab a rice ball of my own, taking a bite, willing the thought to go away. But it comes with vengeance along with the voice of my mother.

You can't love her silently. You must love her loudly, openly.

"Um Kaito, is . . . is Hikari alright?" She asks nervously, as though she didn't have the right to ask the question..

"Oh yeah, she seems quite alright." Kaito answers her, offering a smile what I think was for sympathy. "I dropped her off at her house. But I'll pick her up again tomorrow so she can see your Mom again. Do you want me to do anything?"

"No." She shook her head, fiddling with her fingers. "Thank you. For taking care of her."

"Don't worry about it. Do you wanna drive home?"

"No." I answered, handing Kaya her own Onigiri to make her stop fidgeting with her fingers. She was going to rip her nails off her finger soon. "I'll take her back."

"Ah, I apologise Your Highness, I have forgotten my place. But fair warning, I'm staying for dinner."

"C-can I stay for dinner?" She turns to face me, "I miss Ane-san's food."

"She wants you here. If you want to stay for dinner or stay overnight, she'd be overjoyed." I tell her. This was true. If my mother could, she would keep her in her pockets.

"I knew it. I'm her favorite son!" Kaito exclaims. I have no idea how his mind works.

Kaya chuckles and I could visibly see the tension easing off from her. She brings the rice ball to her lips and takes a bite, sighing audibly.

"These are so good." She mutters before taking another bite, and then another.

Whether she was eating the breakfast I made her this morning or the late lunch, I realised I enjoyed watching her eat. There was something so satisfying about her fuelling and nourishing herself with real food, instead of those drugs and alcohol and calling that a day.

Keeping her inside these walls or the walls of the log house was not entirely possible. Just like me, she was the eldest child and with that came responsibilities of taking care of the younger siblings. It was a lifelong task and while I didn't need to do much to fulfill those duties now, Kaya still did.

But Hikari-chan was now 18 years-old and didn't really need an overbearing older sister.

And there was that birthday celebration for my dear father next week. . . meaning there were many preparations to be done. An extra hand would help my mother.

You may have created some logical explanation for yourself like it was for her benefit but know very well it was for your benefit.

My mother's voice echoes inside my head forcing me to shut my eyes. What a headache.

Something sticky touches my lips and I open my eyes, finding her attempting to shove a rice ball into my mouth.

"You need to eat too." She says, pouting her lips like a child would when they don't get their way. I open my mouth, grabbing a bite of the onigiri that was still in her hands and made my mind.

She will continue to stay by my side for she was mine.

Chapter 14 - Kaya

N ew Chapter!!!

Just a little warning, this chapter is longer than the previos one so again, I recommend you read this chapter when you have more time to read it lesiurely.

Some more Translations you might need

Kumicho/Oyabun - The leader of a Yakuza Organization

Okasan - Mother / Mom

Onichan - Older brother, often used by younger sister

Chan (after a name - e.g. Kaya-chan) - an endearment commonly given to girls

Enjoy your reading time.

"And in the silence I suddenly understood the many ways a person can die still be alive."

- Carmen Rodrigues (34 Pieces of you)

Tiptoeing down the darkly lit staircase, I strain my ears to listen what he was doing at two am in the night, or morning, whatever. For the past four nights I've been here, he's always downstairs doing something or maybe nothing, but I was nosy and wanted to know.

I was supposed to go home. Supposed to talk with my sister and discuss about the whole situation with my mother. The thought makes me squirm from the inside out and leaves a bitter taste in my mouth that never quite disappears fully.

But when given the opportunity to evade that particular mess even for a short while, I took it. Avoiding problems was a skill I was highly competent at though I was not proud of it.

A week, I told myself. After a week I would finish helping out Ane-san with the birthday celebrations for the Oyabun and then I will face with my familial disorder.

"What are you doing?"

I look up, finding Ryo with his glasses on, one hand in his pockets, the other holding his phone as he surveyed me from top to bottom. I was wearing Minori's old shirt and shorts which were slightly big on me, but they were comfortable enough to lounge in.

Pulling away from the hand railing of the stairs I look around the area to buy some time to figure out what I was going to say.

"Uh . . . um . . . I . . ."

"Are you going to stand there all night?" He turns around, placing the phone on the main dining room table that expanded a whole three meters though it rarely gets used before heading to the kitchen, filling up a kettle with tap water then turning it on.

Not knowing whether that was my cue to leave or not, I decided it didn't matter and sat on the kitchen counter stool, brushing my hand up and down my opposite arm. I wasn't cold by any means though the temperature was starting to cool as the days go by, I just needed to something with my hands or fingers to occupy my mind.

With his back still turned to me, he was busy washing something in the sink then dries it with a paper towel and putting it in a small glass bowl. The kettle switches off, steam blowing upwards as he retrieves two cups from the cupboard above him and teabags from a draw that gets placed into the mugs.

"Do you always do this? Making tea at night?" I asked, curiosity getting the better of me.

"Sometimes," he replied, pouring the boiled water into the two mugs before he sets one in front of me with a bowl full of berries and the other in front of him as he takes a seat next to me. "Sometimes sake. Sometimes just water."

"Do you still find it hard to sleep?" I take a raspberry, sighing in contentment as the sour sweet flavour travels in my mouth.

"Yeah." He answers bringing his cup closer to him for a sip but the steam fogs his glasses, halting him momentarily.

A laugh bubbles out from me, finding a man who does illegal business and murder for an occupation, looking like any normal person hilarious. Casting a glance towards him, briefly, I see him smile while taking his glasses off and placing them on the counter. The smile however fleeting its presence was, made him appear youthful and . . . cute.

I take the mug and take a huge gulp to hide whatever face I was making only for the hot drink to burn my tongue.

"Agh!" I yelp.

He chuckles at my miserable existence, shoving a strawberry into my mouth which does help with the burn as I chew on it. I grab another one to soothe the uncomfortable tingling sensation after mumbling, "it's not funny."

"Sure."

"It's not."

"I know."

Huffing from annoyance like a child (I couldn't help myself), I blow down on the cup thoroughly before taking a sip. Lavender tea.

It used to be one of my favourite tea choice. I enjoyed the flowery, earthy flavour that was naturally slightly sweet and comforting. My shoulders relax and my body warms from head to toe. I missed this.

"How are all the plans going along? I know Mom's been bombarding you with all her creative ideas."

A smile finds its way on my lips as I recollect the recent events I had with Ane-san. She involved me with all the preparations from the food and beverages to be served, and chefs to hire, to the minor details like flower arrangements which I personally loved.

"It's going along well," I said, taking another sip.

"I'll be looking forward to it."

And just like that, we settle in comfortable silence, both of us taking sips of our tea and me eating the whole bowl full of strawberries, blueberries, and raspberries. It reminded me of the past where him, Kaito, and I, would sneak out of his room to snack on chips and chocolate in the middle of the night, thinking we got away with it. We didn't. The morning after our small, naughty adventure, we all got a stern warning from Ane-san and promised not to do it again.

We broke the promise. Time and time again. Eventually Ane-san gave up and had the helpers stock our favorite chip flavours (original and barbeque) and bars of chocolates of our choice (I personally loved KitKat's).

We were so happy and naïve back then – or at least I was. Kaito's personality hadn't changed much in all the years I've known him, but he used his goofy nature to hide the small darkness that matched the world we lived in and Ryo, well he was always like this. Reserved, manipulative, stern.

I guess that was why Kaito and him balanced well. They were the polar opposites, yet very similar. Where he was quiet, Kaito was loud. Where his natural aura was frightening, Kaito's was welcoming.

But people shouldn't be fooled by Kaito's welcoming nature. He was just as frightening as Ryo, if not more when provoked badly. But those occasions were rare and far in between and the world should be thankful for that.

Those two were immoral from the start and would entertain any form destruction they pleased. Arson? Child's play. Water boarding? Entertainment. Lengthy tortures? A little boring.

"Go back to bed, even if you can't sleep. Relax your body even if it's just a little. You have a long day ahead." He said, taking his cup and empty bowl to the sink.

"Training with those boys again?" I ask, finishing my tea and placing the cup in the sink as well.

He gives an affirmative nod. Despite his cold disposition, he was quite nurturing in nature and when he told me about the five boys he took in from Japan, I wasn't surprised. He'd be a good father.

Where did that thought come from? No, it was an objective thought, anyone can see that; I reason to myself.

"Go. Rest." He tells me off, before leaving the kitchen and dining area, heading towards the secondary home across the expansive lawn that he called 'the shed', while I stood there still lost in thought.

Guests were streaming through steadily, finger foods were all set, the weather was lovely, and all plans were moving accordingly. A small wave of pride flows subtly within me, and the nerves starts to settle. Maybe I can pull this off.

"The flowers are lovely," Ane-san fondly comments in Japanese, slipping her arm through mine. "It's a great thing you're in the good graces of the Taylor's, especially Alaina. She is a force to beckon with."

"She sure is," I agree.

The whole underworld feared her. She was labelled as the psycho female assassinunderworld for a reason. It was only recently that I met her in the flesh and shocked to see how sweet she was and no she is not psycho, far from it.

We hit it off immediately with our love for flowers and botany and when I requested her for flower arrangements, she happily agreed. You could say the flowers were a gift from the Taylor family.

We walk around the lawn, smiling and briefly greeting the guests as we checked through and ensured all the other arrangements like the chefs we hired were ready to prepare to feast the guests and the instrumentalist where comfortable to perform.

"You've done an excellent job Kaya-chan." She squeezes my hand, smiling brightly. "I knew you were good at these things."

My brain freezes for a moment. Was she complimenting me?

"Oh dear, don't cry." She dabs gently underneath my eye with a handkerchief before pulling me into her embrace, holding me tightly. "You deserve the compliments. You are doing well. Believe my words."

I nod in response, scared to say anything. I didn't deserve her or her compliments.

She pulls away slowly, looking me in the eye.

"It takes time to heal but you'll get there, I promise." She takes my hands and hold it in hers, "I believe in you." Smiling, she gives me another in the hands before walking away to where the Oyabun was standing, waiting for her.

I admired their relationship, silent but true. I've never heard them exchange words of love, but they loved each other so much. It was the way he would wrap his arms around her possessively but affectionately. The way he would only look at Ane-san even when focused on a conversation with someone else entirely. The way she would smile every time her eyes meets his. The way they would only look for each other within a crowd.

Love like theirs was so passionate and honest.

"Look who's shamelessly walking around the Oyabun's lawn after the mess her father has caused." An annoyingly familiar voice remarks. I didn't need to turn around and entertain them. I stay rooted in my spot, summoning all the calm I had.

No need to react, I tell myself. No need.

"She's just as much as a traitor as her father. If I were her, I would be to ashamed to even step foot here," another comments.

"Agreed. I would be too mortified." They all laugh, loud and pretentious.

"I think the one who should be ashamed and mortified are you. Do you need a lecture? Or should I get rid of you once and for all?" A deceptively calm voice filters through, silencing the group immediately.

"M-Minori-san. Greetings." Akane, the first girl stammers, her face looking pale all of a sudden.

"Go. Now," was all Minori bothered to say, and the group of girls leave, pulling each other along.

She shakes her head, muttering something under her breath before approaching me. "No need to listen them. Their heads are practically empty." She hands me a glass of champaign, clinking our glasses before elegantly taking a sip. "I heard you prepared all of this with Okasan. I am impressed."

"It was a joint effort and she guided me through everything."

"No need to undermine yourself. I know effort when I see it." She takes another sip of her glass before placing it down on the cloth covered table. "By the way, you look beautiful today."

I look down at my dark navy dress that blended in with everyone else.

"The one shoulder is giving. Elegant and bold. I love it."

"Thank you. You look gorgeous as always." I admire her black maxi dress with sheer long sleeves that split a little under the elbow delivering a flowy feel that seamlessly compliments the sharp features of the dress in itself. "Oh, and sorry, I've been borrowing your clothes."

"Oh I know, Onichan told me. Use whatever you like." She leans in close, whispering into my ear, "Ryo has hoodies and jumpers in his wardrobe, third draw on the left." She winks before nodding to someone behind me.

"What are you conspiring now?"

"A little mischief," she replied going to him for a hug. Unsurprisingly, Ryo openly hugs her back and my heart fills with cuteness overload, their sibling relationship was adorable to put it plainly. But even so, a faint sense of jealousy and envy passes by.

"You look pretty," he compliments after pulling away from each other. "Another dress from the collection?"

"Mhmm," she affirms, "wardrobe of my dreams." Her eyes seemed to glow as she spoke and rightfully so. Her now fiancé, the Pakhan of the States Bratva, created a whole wardrobe for her with everything she needed, from casual wear to formal wear, she explained there was everything.

Speaking of the devil.

"There you are," Nikolai Fedorov plants a kiss on Minori's forehead adoringly as he wraps his arms around her waist. Amongst the Japanese crowd he stood out immensely as the only Caucasian with very intense blue eyes and towering build. The majority of us looked more like dwarfs compared to him.

"You took a while." Minori comments smiling broadly. Similarly to her brother, Minori wasn't one to express her emotions openly so seeing her smiling without care or caution was new and refreshing. I was happy for her for that.

"Talking with your father sure does take a while," he explained before nodding to Ryo and myself in greeting. "How's it going little bro?"

"I am not your bro."

"Soon you will."

"I will not."

I try my very hardest to hold back a laugh, but this was hilarious. Besides Kaito, no one talks to Ryo like that. Minori always said that her brother was the closest thing to a fox. In Japanese folklore, fox's are able to transform and disguise themselves into things they are not. For Ryo, it was appearing friendly and approachable. It was a manipulative tactic for people to think that he is willing to say yes to anything when in truth by that point, he already had you in his palms.

So for him to reveal his true self and show genuine disgust and annoyance without the desire to eliminate the person was extraordinary.

"Stop it both of you." Minori jokingly scolds, frowning at Nikolai. "I'll see you later Onichan. And you too Kaya."

"If he gets too annoying, you can come back."

Minori laughs at her brother's comment, waving before the couple retreats to the background filled with guests and important members of the organization.

"Mom was very pleased with everything you planned. She said you were a genius."

What about you? What do you think?

"She's too kind."

"Father was quite satisfied too," he added. "Satisfaction is the closest thing you'll get to impressed from him."

But what about you?

"I will have to properly greet him later. The last I saw him; he was too busy with Ane-san and other people."

"You'll get a chance. And even if the opportunity don't arise, he'll call for you. He's been wanting to talk to you for a while."

Well, that is . . . interesting.

Ryo was manipulative, no questions asked. But his father? He was a whole new level. No, new levels. He treated most people like objects rather than living things and as long as the event moves accordingly to his favor, he couldn't care less about the losses. The loss could involve lives and as long as it wasn't his wife and children (No, actually, not even his children were excluded. Minori almost died last year but he knew how the events will fold out and doesn't seriously entertain the idea of losing his children) he could use anyone's life as an interesting factor and watch how the situation pans out.

Yes, he didn't hate me and liked me cursing his son out, but I wasn't safe.

In the distance, a scream pierces through the chattering guests as a shot rings in the air, silencing us all. It was followed by many more. Consecutively. Again and again.

People either froze or ran towards the estate for cover.

Ryo grabs my arm, pulling me behind him. Taking out his gun from his breast pocket, he surveys the area, finding for the culprit. Then, he was yelling at someone or multiple people to do something, but I could only hear more shots being fired. I didn't know whether those shots were from the attacker's side or ours.

Men and women were yelling for the rest of us to get inside but soon the consequences of those shots were becoming evident. People were falling down, blood splattering. Most of the blood smeared the green grass but at times, it marked the faces of those nearby.

This . . . this wasn't the first time something like this happened. I've seen this before.

I briefly registered that I was running, following the lead of Ryo as he pulled me. We weren't running towards the estate or the secondary home. We were running towards the storage shed. I could sense the rising panic as my breath began to come in short, rapid burst with my chest started to burn.

Please, please don't put me in there.

"Stay here." He shoves me inside, closing the door on my face.

Trapping me and my past unintentionally, again.

Chapter 15 - Kaya and Ryo

Ｎew Chapter!!!

This chapter is written in two POVs - first the Narrator, narrating Kaya's past, then Ryo's POV. There are also flashback in Ryo's POV which are italicised. The POV's are bolded/italicised but please be careful when reading the different POV's so you don't confuse yourself.

Warning: murder and death are detailed in this chapter. Please take of yourself and read what is most comfortable for you.

Hey guys, another chapter two days in a row. I just really wanted to post this chapter and couldn't keep it so here you go. ▢▢▢

But there is more angst coming our way so you are warned (hehehe I love angst)

Anyways, enjoy reading.

"Tell me anything. Tell me nothing. I will listen. Even when you have nothing but silence to offer. I will still listen."

- Lucas W

Kaya aged 7 years – Narrator's POV

"Do you learn nothing!?" Kaya's father roared, striking his daughter in the face causing her to collapse onto the hard tiled floor. Kaya doesn't get a moment to recollect herself before her father grabs her wrist, gripping it tight, his nails digging into her skin. Like all the times he laid hands on her, this was sure to become another mark similar to the rest. "Do you only know how to be a disappointment!?"

Akio Hashimoto was a frightening man. Anger wasn't required to instil fear, his mere presence does just that. Consequently, he rarely displayed emotions, much less anger. But when provoked, he was horrifying in every sense of the word.

"I'm sorry!" Kaya begs in apology, trying to pull away from her father. From the retaliation he only looks down at her, his eyes red and bulging. His hands pull away from her arm before reaching her neck, slamming her against the nearest wall.

"You will learn to be sorry," he mouths, tightening his hold on her neck, closing her windpipe slowly before abruptly letting go and dragging her down the corridor.

Kaya could only close her mouth, bite the insides of her cheeks, and face the consequences of her father's wrath. There was absolutely nothing that could stop her father now, she knew.

They stop in front of a seemingly normal door she knew and hated. Her father opens it with no patience before shoving her inside with such force that resulted in Kaya pummelling onto the cold wooden floor, pain radiating on her right side.

"You will stay here until you learn your lesson." The door shuts in front of her before she had the chance to apologise once more, the familiar metal clinking sound of the locks being put in place filters through followed by harsh footsteps receding into the background.

She knew anything she did now would be pointless. If she yelled for her father, it would only be met with more beatings, more lessons to be learnt. It left her with more pain, more wounds, and later on more scars. More reminders of how unloving and pathetic her existence was.

The storage room was located in the basement and was cold throughout the year but was especially harsh during the winter. The room had no windows, no lights, no bathroom, no blankets, no water, or food. All that existed was unending darkness, unwelcoming cold, and the promise of ruination. Here she would have to spend two days alone if her father were generous or up to a week with a cup of water delivered to her from the third morning. Nothing else.

Kaya backed into her usual corner, cradling her knees, rocking back and forth, closing her eyes and imagined a place better.

A beach house, a paradise. Clear waters, beautiful sunsets, laughter. A rainforest. Abundant in greenery and peace. A zoo. Loud animals, quiet animals, all of them adorable.

'Think,' she told herself. 'More good places!'

But her mind always returned to the storage room she was in, dark and ominous. There was nothing there she knew, but something was creeping up on her, ready to surround her, harm her, suffocate her.

She pulls on her hair, relishing the momentary pain and distraction.

'More,' she thought.

So she pulled harder, tighter. Ripping the first few strands of hair. It felt blissful. She did it again and again and again. But as she reaches up to do it once more, it didn't feel right.

Shocked and frightened, she brought her hands closer to her chest, fiddling with them. Then she brought her nails to mouth biting on them. Then she picks on them. Then she bites on them again.

'Off, I want them off,' she thought.

And ripped them off.

Small trickle of blood bubbled on the surface, and she felt pain. Reassuring pain.

Pain inflicted by others hurt. It gripped her and left unwanted marks. But pain she realised, inflicted by herself was okay. She had a choice in that matter. It wasn't necessarily against her will.

Pain she inflicted on herself was a release. It felt good, soothing even. In that moment, when she hurt herself, everything was placed in the background, hazy and irrelevant.

She wasn't in the storage room. Her father wasn't striking her. She wasn't going crazy.

The darkness wasn't suffocating her. It wasn't haunting her. It wasn't affecting her.

It wasn't. It wasn't. It wasn't.

It was.

RYOSUKE - present

I didn't care for what my father was ordering us to do or whatever else people were doing. With blood splattered onto my clothes, the grass on the lawns, the walls, dead people, enemies, and ally, littered on the floor, some with their eyes still open, there was plenty of issues to be cleared and information needed to be gathered but I did not care for it at all.

Making haste, I run back towards the storage room, shrugging off my jacket suit and throwing it somewhere.

I jerk the door open, sunlight seeping into the darkness of the unused room. And I find her. Curled up, knees to her chest as she gasped for each breath, tears streaming down her face. She seemed to have been fiddling with her fingers but her nail from her index finger was missing.

"Kaya." I step forward into the room, though she doesn't take notice. "Kaya, look."

She flinches, whimpering as she backs away from me, her back hitting the wall.

"P-please don't, d-don't hurt me," she pleads in a hushed tone, her voice hitching as she fought the sobs to say the words.

I remember myself in that same position, begging for the whole thing to be over. Begging for the torture my father thought necessary for my education. A lesson he would say.

"I won't hurt you," I begin to say raising my hands in the air where she could see and backing away slowly towards the door. "I will never hurt you."

It was clear she wasn't rational in thought, and she was seeing illusions from her past. One I didn't know. One I should've known. Those small little habits should've been obvious. The fiddling with her fingers, the way she often bit the inside of her cheeks, the way she pulled on her hair when she was lost in thought.

I was too blinded by her chatty, bubbly aura to care what existed underneath. I only assumed that all those attempts, all those blank faces, the changes were a result of her brother's death.

But maybe, that was only the trigger.

Maybe, she never wanted to live.

I was now completely out of the room, just in front of the entrance. She watches my every step, her breaths still ragged but beginning to settle faintly.

"Kaya, it's me." I crouch down, to her eye level. "Ryo."

A flash of clarity shines in her eyes before she whispers, "Ryo?"

"Yeah. That's me."

A sob comes out of her, more tears welling in her eyes. She reaches her arms out and I don't think even for a second. By the time I knew it, my arms were firmly wrapped around her frame, her head against my chest, relief slowly calming me down.

"I-I don't l-like dark rooms," she wails, her words getting caught up from the tears, sobs and coughs that wracked her body.

"I'm sorry. I'm sorry. I'm sorry." I kiss the side of her face. "It won't happen again."

"P-promise?"

"Promise." I affirm. Her body relaxes marginally, and I take it as a sign to get her out of here. Scooping her body, I bring her as close as possible to me, placing her head into the crook of my neck a hand on her eyes. She didn't need to see the scene.

Ignoring anyone who passed by, I headed towards the car park, placing her into the passenger seat and drove off.

Carrying her inside, I turn the lights on.

I head towards the bathroom, setting her on the counter and grabbing the first aid kit.

Urge told me to keep her close to me. Hold her longer, tighter. But logic knew there were tasks to be done.

Taking her left hand and inspecting her index finger, I grab the disinfectant solution, dab it on some sterile gauze, patting it onto her bare nail bed. Her face scrunches from the pain for a second before she got used to the stinging pain.

Drying off the excess disinfectant, I put on some Vaseline and cover it with a bandage. My hands stay put holding hers, unwilling to let go.

"Can I take bath?" she asks, her face not meeting mine.

"Yeah." I answer, releasing her hand. I move to leave the room when she grabs hold of the cuff of my shirt.

"Stay," she mumbles, her face looking down on the tiled floors. "I don't want to be alone."

"Okay."

She gets off the counter, taking the plug and wedging it in the drain before turning on the taps. The hot water rushes out, steadily filling the tub as she turns around to face me.

"You said there's nothing you haven't seen in regard to my body." She begins to unzip her dress. "You're wrong." The dress unveils from her body, pooling at her feet. "But I haven't seen yours either. Not fully."

She takes off her undergarments, shame free then dips her legs into the water before dropping her body underneath the water.

The tap continued to run, reaching just about halfway with her in it.

It was a dare of sorts. A challenge. An opportunity.

I could only see a portion of her back and the left side of her body but already, I could see her skin being marred with all kinds of scars. Majority of them old, some faded. Many of them were scars I was familiar with. While others I could identify were inflicted by her.

Scars marked by abuse were ugly and flawed. Scars marked by the need to feel something were often clean and strategic.

Starting with unbuttoning my shirt, I take off every piece of clothing before sinking into the water. She watched me as I do so, remaining impassive.

I turn off the taps, the tub now full.

She leans in close, as though to inspect something. Her eyes widen, lips pursuing as she retreats away from me. She looks away from me, but I could see her face reddening, tears welling, and she was biting the inside of her cheeks again.

"You did it again." She says after she seemed to settle herself. But her face remained away from mine. "Covering my eyes. It's happened before, right? About 20 years ago? When we were children?"

I grab her hand and push her underneath one of the cloth covered tables as the sound of bullets being shot rang in the air, one after another.

Covering her body with my own, I place both my hands one her eyes just before a body collapses onto the ground. Blood was slowly spreading outwards from her chest as her head lolled towards us, staring blankly.

"I couldn't see what happened, but I could hear it. It was just like today. Lots of shooting, screaming, yelling. But none of that really bothered me." She turns to face me. "Because the thing I heard over all that noise was your voice, telling me to be quiet. I felt safe. Even if we were powerless, useless kids." She leans in closer towards me.

"The only reason I forgot about that was because . . . I guess it was a defence mechanism after what I saw."

Shots continued to fire, Otosan was yelling orders and people ran about. My heart thundered inside my chest, but I couldn't show signs of weakness.

Another man falls, his weapon sliding under the table.

A gun.

I've seen Otosan and other people using it and understood the general idea of how to use it but I never actually ever used it before. Regardless, using my legs, I gather the weapon closer to me, just in case.

The commotion continues as she trembled underneath me. But she didn't cry and just like I told her, she hasn't made a single sound.

From a distance I see combat boots walking towards us. Closer and closer.

For a moment I closed my eyes in foolish hope that if I kept them closed, it would disappear. Realising my stupidity I open them. Now those shoes were inches away from us.

"Keep your eyes closed." I whisper into Kaya's ears as I grab the weapon and hold it like I've seen Otosan do. The weapon was so heavy in my hold and my arm trembled with the weight of it.

The cloth covering the table folds above, and the face with the ugliest smirk appears. He laughs at me, shaking his head.

I pull the trigger.

Time stops for a second, then restarts as the smirk disappears from his face and he falls gradually on his back. Then stays on the floor, unmoving. Still, frozen.

The weapon falls from my hands.

Kaya was staring back at me.

"Our brains are so sensitive and delicate and I suppose for four-year-old me, I couldn't . . . process it. So the next best thing was to forget about it."

It wasn't too difficult to accept an adult in a world full of bloodshed to be a murderer. The same couldn't be said for a child. No child should be capable of it, much less be proud of it. She would now think I was a monster.

However, should the same situation occur again, I would still pull the trigger. I would still kill them. It was a better alternative than dying by some scum or have her dead. That wasn't ever an acceptable choice. So if she sees me as a monster, so be it. I didn't care. That was who I was.

Her hands reaches outwards, planting against my left cheek.

"Thank you," she smiles. "For protecting me."

Her thumb sweeps under my eye. I couldn't understand her. It was . . . irrational. Normal people would run away. Normal people should be horrified. So why . . . why was she smiling and still here?

"It was stupid of me to think that I know everything about you. But you are warned, I will. With time."

"So will I." I reply, planting my own hand against her hand still on my face. She was still the Kaya I knew but there was more to her.

But that was okay. More of her only meant more parts to adore.

I liked the thought.

Chapter 16 - Kaya

N ew Chapter

Warning: Mentions of abuse, negative self-talk and self-harm are explored within this chapter. It can be a very sensitive topic so please take care of yourselves and read what you are comfortable reading.

Sorry for not posting for a while got a little busy these days but I am back and I will try to upload more chapters, more consistently.

I'm not sure why but it seems this story is full of lengthy chapters and this one is again, another one of them. So, like always, I recommend reading this chapter when you have extra time on you.

But for now, I hope you enjoy this chapter

It's hard to fight with intangible battles, but it's even harder to pretend everything's fine when things are just falling apart.

- Areeba

It never occurred to me how much satisfaction I would feel in this moment where I see him with his eyes closed for a prolonged period of time.

His hair was freshly washed by yours truly after he offered to wash mine. I should've known he was capable of many more domestic activities given that he had cared for his sister for all of his life but this caring side of him was a quality of his I admired. His face was absent of the constant frown he wore like armour and his skin was unsurprisingly flawless up close.

I have never seen Ryo sleep. Not when we I was a cheeky five year old, not when I was a moody teenager, or a depressed adult. I came to a conclusion early in my adolescence that he most likely suffered from insomnia. Whether that was something he always had or because of some circumstances, it didn't change the fact that he was unable to rest or replenish his body even after all the strenuous tasks he has to do.

For a long time, I was much too self-centred to care about it. Far too deep with my own issues when in reality they weren't that big of a deal. Children receive punishments when they commit incorrect actions. People, family members, die. We all die.

The only choice we are given, is to either express your hardship or to keep them to yourself.

I chose to self-destruct openly, while he, chose to lock it up and hide them.

All along I thought we were the complete opposites. Me being extroverted, open, and annoying, while he was introverted, silent, and was out of everyone's way. But now I realise despite our differences there were similarities. We were alike in so many aspects of our lives we chose to ignore it. Because what good would it bring to dig and find our scars, our pasts, our fears?

Pain. Shame. Embarrassment.

It highlighted our weakness. Giving evidence to our vulnerability - how fragile, powerless, defective we were.

I couldn't be sure as to how he thought about his own scars but I hated them, especially the ones marked by my father. I had no control over what happened to my body, my mind. I had no control in stopping it or preventing the situation from happening in the first place.

And they never leave. Some fade but most don't. And they never leave my damaged brain. At times, particularly in the night, they replay over and over and over again, trapping me with memories I longed to forget.

What was worse was that I needed the pain like a drug addict. Without the pain I could not function. Without the pain all the thoughts that are usually whispers increase in volume and begin to scream in my ear.

No one cares about you!

You are a useless fool!

You're a disappointment! You should have never been born! No one wanted you!

And so I peeled off my nails, pulled out my hair, slit my wrists, my thighs, my stomach, any piece of skin accessible to my damaged mind that will quiet the voices. They could never be silenced but I accepted that long ago.

I relished in the pain, giving a moment of reprieve.

I enjoyed seeing the dark crimson liquid that poured reminding me I was still human - that I could feel something.

My mind wanders as my fingers trace his intricate tattoos on his left arm, trace his scars, his pain that hid beneath it. Concealing the past, trapping the present.

Did it hurt?

Did he feel lonely? Did he feel pain?

Does he need pain like I do?

"Still busy gawking?" His eyes flutter open, much too nicely and I am reminded how long his lashes were. Why did men have longer, more beautiful looking lashes than us women? It was not fair.

"Yes." I say hoping to sound unapologetic but only ended up sounding as though I was choking on my own saliva.

"Hmm." He answers, turning on his side, bringing me closer to him, my head against his chest, his heart thumping regularly, unaffected, contrary to mine. "Sleep. There is much to do tomorrow."

I did not want to think of what laid ahead tomorrow. There was no doubt a lot of cleaning was involved, metaphorically.

"Do you have an idea who was behind the event?" I questioned, curious.

"I don't know." He admits, brushing his fingers through my hair that was in much need of a haircut. "My father may have an idea but all of that can wait till tomorrow."

As much of an Empire the Sakurazauki-gumi was, the bigger the organization, the more enemies you have. There was no such thing as exceptions. And I didn't need to think to know that the Oyabun had truckloads of them.

The cleaning was to be difficult I was sure.

"What do you want me to do? My task, I mean." I clarify.

"We can talk about that tomorrow." He pulls on the comforter, ensuring that it covered me fully. "Close your eyes for now."

"I'm too awake for it."

"Speak with your eyes closed then."

Closing my eyes, my other senses heighten. The smell of freshly washed sheets that were definitely dried in the bright sunshine, his clean citrus minty scent, the feel of his even breath fanning ever so slightly on my hair, his heartbeat regular and bounding, the rise and fall of his chest, the warmth, his assurance, the calm - the safety.

Feeling childish but not having the energy to care, I snuggle closer to him, basking my self in the safety and warmth his presence provides and not wanting any of it to end.

In response, like I was his child, he pats my back in a regular beat, lulling me to sleep. My eyes begin droop as the tension from my body seeps out, my mind quiet, silent.

"Good night." I last hear him whisper in my ear with a kiss.

A heated debate rumbles on as the high-ranking men of the organization in their crisp black suits screams what they believe should be done from the catastrophe that occurred less than 24 hours ago.

Inside the gorgeously furnished but severely impersonal meeting room, some claimed to find those responsible immediately and deal with them - they were the hot-headed ones without extra knowledge to know that there would be consequences in those actions. There was always a reason for a massacre to occur without trace. Bulldozing recklessly would only get more of us killed and stain our organization from how stupid we all were.

The other, smarter ones asserted to tread carefully and determine what their full intentions were. Or more specifically what they wanted to achieve by annihilating our organization knowing they wouldn't be able to touch the Oyabun or their heir.

A few thought it was caused by the now notorious MeX organization which my own father was affiliated with. They all look towards direction with dirty glances but didn't have the courage to outwardly express their disgust in front of the Oyabun who spared myself and my family. That was the thing about them, they were cowards and never wanted to appear different from others.

But the thought of it being MeX was quickly disregarded since they always left notes when they were approaching. Always left clues as though they wanted to be found - almost like they were doing this for fun, although no one would have agreed with what I thought.

The Oyabun sat at the top seat, his posture relaxed making no move to verbalise anything, appearing nonchalant as usual. But those who knew him well, knew that people and organizations making a move on his own organization was a thrill he was happy to entertain. Well, that was as long as his wife was not personally involved which was a fortunate thing for whoever or whatever the organization was responsible. If that were the case, this whole situation would have been settled last night with more blood and more bodies - dead bodies.

I sat sandwiched between Ryo and Kaito, the only woman in this god forsaken meeting room despite many accusations and concerns which were effectively ignored when Ryo shut them up and the Oyabun seemed disinterested in their concerns. But a part of me wished I was dismissed from this room so I could spend some time with Ane-san and maybe eat her food and not be in the middle of a room riled with pure testosterone.

Looking to my left, Kaito was tuned into the conversation, no doubt curating a list in his mind and mapping out a plan while Ryo on my right began tapping on the mahogany table with his index finger, counting down the time until he was ready to silence them.

Tap. Tap. Tap.

"Quiet."

The arguments automatically ceases, those standing immediately sits down, their attention now strictly onto the heir. Waiting to see if their pleads were heard.

"Men and women have died yesterday. Like always we will repay them as deserved and more." Ryo pauses, glancing his father's way before returning his attention to his men. "But this was a carefully planned attack and I have no intention of rushing. Weeding the issue from the root is always better."

Some men swallow while others remain impassive.

Tap. Tap. Tap.

"Utilize everything you have at your dispense to gather clues and information and bring them forward. We will begin by painting the full picture."

"Then we can finish them?" Tanaka, a guy as hotblooded and carnivorous as a human could be questioned with an awfully hideous smirk on his face. Though I must admit he was loyal, he was more like a wild animal than human. He was more interested in a bloodbath than tactics.

"Yes." Ryo answers unfazed, his deep mellow voice travelling across the room.

A collective murmur in agreement settles in the room as some are satisfied with the plan while other's not so much. But none of that matters. The issue at hand was settled.

"You are dismissed." Oyabun orders promptly, we all bow down at a respectful 90 degrees before the men slowly drifted out of the room in silence until they were completely outside and began to chat amongst themselves like teenage girls with gossip that must be shared.

While some leave immediately, other lingers around the communal space of this expansive mansion, immersed into conversation.

Kaito and Ryo pays no mind, walking down the corridor to the East wing of mansion. I follow like a puppy on a leash, the smell of home cooked food greeting us as the familiar affectionate hug envelops me tight.

"I'm glad you're safe." Ane-san tells me in Japanese, her subtle floral scent drifting around her. "Now show me your face." She loosens her hold on me, palming my face in her hands. I offer a smile.

"I'm fine. I'm glad you're safe too." I say, my thoughts genuine.

"Ane-san, I thought I was your favorite son!" Kaito pouts, begging for attention.

"Yes, yes." Ane-san nods, patting his head while her true son was seated on the kitchen counter, pouring himself tea.

She takes mine and Kaito's hand whisking us too to the kitchen counter, ushering us to take a seat as she set to work preparing steamy bowls of rice, miso soup, and crispy pork katsu with thinly sliced cabbage on the side.

There's a reason why this household didn't have personal chefs though they had helpers of every other kind.

We all thank for the food and begin eating, Kaito and I sagging with delight with the crispy salty meaty taste of the pork katsu dancing across our tongues while annoyingly so, Ryo ate quietly, sophisticatedly. Nostalgia and longing creeps up and now we were all young children again, waiting for lunch to be served, our tiny mouths stuffed with Ane-san's cooking.

I soak in the memory while eating, an odd but welcoming sense of fondness claiming me. I don't even realise Ane-san took a seat next to me until she was talking.

"I received a message," she began, looking at no where in particular. "From your mother."

I swallow hard on my food, almost choking myself. She hands me a cup of tea and I gulp in down. Of course my mother would know who to text to force me to do something.

"She wanted to speak to you. Privately." She looks at me knowingly. "I told her you would come, in your own time. When you're ready."

"Thank you." I whispered.

"I don't want to push you to do anything you don't want to do."

"But?" I ask sensing there was more.

"But you don't have a lot of time. I don't want you to regret anything."

I take this in knowing she was right. As much as I was a professional at avoiding problems, nothing worthwhile comes out of it. Especially not this kind. Problems were like unattended wounds that would fester and become infected and spread without prompt interventions.

"I seem to always avoid my problems until I'm forced to meet them in the eye." I admit, knowing she would never judge me for it. She has always been more of a mother than my biological one.

"The problems you face are not easy. Not even for grown adults with many life experiences." She pulls in close bringing my head closer to hers.

"But if there is one quality about you that sets you apart from others, it is your resilience. You struggle, you get hurt, you might avoid problems, but eventually you work out a way to go through with your problems. Not everyone is capable of that."

My insides knot and squirm knowing I was nothing like she described me to be. I always tried to find the easy way out.

I wasn't resilient. I was pathetic.

I was deceiving her. I was fake.

"It's okay to struggle," she went on. "To feel pain, to want to give up. That does not make you any less of a person. In fact, that makes you real. Strong in your own right."

"Not everyone will agree." I said toying with my cup.

"Not everyone is brave enough to admit they're struggling," she stated eyeing me carefully.

Silence settles beside the two guys who continued to eat their food.

"I'll go," I decided, the words tasting bitter on my tongue. "Better late than never. Right?"

She gives a satisfied nod and a proud smile. "Good girl. Now finish off your food."

I didn't have much of an appetite left with the heavy conversation draining me completely but eat it anyway, thinking more about the taste rather than the whole eating, chewing, swallowing part.

The two guys sitting to my left acts as they normally do, with Kaito attempting to steal a cutlet of Ryo's katsu while he shoves Kaito in the ribs.

They both pretended nothing happened and no conversation occurred. It was easier that way and I was thankful for that.

Soaking up this little piece of normalcy and comfort, I finish my food preparing for what was to come.

Chapter 17 - Kaya

New Chapter!!!

Warning: Ideas of suicidal thoughts and psychological/physical abuse are explored within this chapter. Please take care of yourselves and read what is most comfortable for you.

Just a little note for the eldest daughter's and son's: Your efforts in helping raise your younger siblings never truly go unnoticed. They see it and it might not feel like it, but everything you do try and make your siblings life better than yours is appreciated. You are worthy of praise and admiration. □

Without   further   ado,   enjoy   your   reading   time.
□□---

I am a differen person to different people.

Annoying to one. Talented to another. Quiet to a few. Unknown to a lot.

But who am I, to me?

- Unknown

Despite the clear weather and radiant sunlight beaming through, it was anything but bright in this four-walled room. Like opium drugs I was certain she was on, it smelt of dying and despair - any and all semblance of hope destroyed, and it felt much too familiar for my liking. All I wanted to do from the second I stepped foot into this room was to get out - immediately.

My feet halts after entering a few inches inside, rejecting the idea to go in any further.

"You came." My mother's raspy voice called as she tried to prop herself up into a sitting position, failing miserably. From the time I've seen her last in the home, she lost more weight, her face emaciated, her skin paper like and fragile.

My legs and arms move before my head, assisting her to sit up right, her skin cold against mine. She heaves in a deep breath her hands planted against her chest, shaking slightly, exhausted from that move alone.

"You said you wanted to talk." I said while grabbing a chair.

"I did." She whispered, her face not meeting mine even as I take a seat to meet her eye level. "There is something you should know."

"What did you want to tell me?"

"I didn't know how to feel when I had you. A part of me was overjoyed that you were born safe and healthy. Just grateful because I had a few miscarriage before I had you." She sighs like the thought pains her. "But a part of me hated you."

Because I was a girl and not a male heir like my father wanted - the unsaid words rang in my head.

"He said you are nothing more than a failed experiment. And I was his greatest disappointment." She mumbled, staring at the windows.

Her words send dull blades digging into my chest, brutally forcing its way through, but it was nothing new. We both knew that. When Kenji died, my father's hand got harsher, faster. It reached deeper and my mother wasn't safe either. We all came out with bruises larger than our own hands. Split lips, burnt skin, broken bones.

I wasn't just a failure in my existence. I was defective. Like a tech gadget that works but never performs well enough. Useless in it's design, a waste product to be dumped or used for the wrong reasons.

"I knew he slept around with other women." She jumps in thought, her voice flat and devoid emotions like anger or jealousy that would normally lace those words. "But none of them were important to him even if they produced kids. Most of them were girls anyway. And yet, he doted on one of them. So much so he went out of his way to meet them as often as he could and even took care of the children she produced."

Memories of my father leaving the home for weeks at a time resurfaces in my mind. Those times were the best weeks of my life. My wounds healed and I was free. I could still remember praying religiously every night, looking out of my window, hoping he would just stay wherever he was and never come back.

All those prayers were futile. He always came back.

"They had a son and a daughter; they would be about 22 and 20 years old by now. Or maybe a year or two younger. He was so proud of them you know. Always compared them with Kenji and Hikari. He hated all of you. All of us." She stressed the words like that information held great importance, instead of the fact that I could have several half-siblings because my father was a whore.

But another thought barges its way in my mind.

Do those two children know that their father is dead? Did they even know what organization he was affiliated with? Do they know the dangers associated with having a father like that?

"The son is looking for him. His name is Koki if I remember correctly. He'll eventually find you, one way or another."

I couldn't tell if this was a sweet heads up or a threat.

"Don't trust him, ever." She warned, her eyes suddenly sharp. "If he's anything like his father, it's that he has no emotions. No true ones. Just the visceral need to be better than everyone else. To have more than everyone else."

"He could be like us," I attempted to reason. "Emotional and weak."

"Do you truly believe that man would have doted on children that resembled you? Emotional and weak like you?" She questioned her tone harsh on the ears, coming out more like an accusation.

I swallow hard realising she was right. Father hated all of us. I was his first greatest disappointment being a girl. Kenji was his second disappointment realising his soft nature that resembled no part of him. Hikari was the third disappointment because you guessed it, she's a girl. And my mother had to deal with all of this. Smiling in public, acting the part of a doting wife, mother when in private she was treated worse than those living on streets.

We all wore a mask in the public, pretending and deceiving. Our walls built thicker and higher to protect ourselves and hid it with a bright smile, good humour, and fake laughs.

"I'll be careful." I settled to say.

"Love isn't real Kaya. It's an artificial emotion people label when they're comfortable. No one will love you."

But love is real, I wanted to scream. I've seen it.

Have you really? Is everything you see real?

Your own parents never loved you, how will anyone else love you?

He can never love you.

"...I know." I answered, swallowing the bitter taste of truth and reality. I almost laughed.

Just a couple of days living blissfully had turned me optimistic for something. Maybe a life, maybe the future. This was the reality check I needed. I don't have a life that's worth achieving anything nor a future worth attempting. If the last 25 years of my life is an indication of anything, it was that any endeavours in trying to make life good was pointless. It was either went unnoticed, ignored or rewarded with hair pulling and a shoving to the ground.

Love was a fantasy. You could read about it, imagine it, dream about it but it would never exist in real life. Love was just a stronger word for affection, comfort or stability. Not something so emotionally potent that it leaves people unable to breathe without one another.

Even if such thing did exist, I've done nothing in my life to deserve it. I let people down and ruin their lives. I was born into this world broken, cracked on the inside. And those cracks were growing larger, spreading further. I won't have undamaged parts left soon.

Perhaps before my deranged mind break me, the innate defective side of me would kill me first. It didn't matter which was first. The only thing that mattered was that one will finish me.

"Was there anything else you wanted to talk about?" I asked, my urge in wanting to leave this room enlarging by the second that ticked by. Like a balloon expanding with air with every exhale, stretching so far it explodes.

"No. But bring Hikari. I want to talk to her. She's so different from you or Kenji." Her rambles become distant to my ears as my chair skids against the floor while I get up.

Smarter than you. Because you are empty headed and stupid.

Brighter than you. Because you never do anything worth noting about.

Better than you. Because you're not capable enough to achieve something worthwhile.

"Onee-chan?" Hikari's hand softly grabs my shoulder. Her light brown eyes that we shared flashed with concern, her brows furrowed. It's been a while since she's called me that. Big sister.

"Moth -, your mother wanted to speak with you. She's waiting inside." I stated, keeping my eyes down on the floor, breathing deeply.

"She can wait. You're acting weird." She pointed out, trying to meet my eye.

"I was never normal, was I?" I released a sarcastic laugh. "Oh wait, I was trying to be Ms perfect in your eyes, wasn't I?" I throw back the words she said two weeks ago, it's trace vile and coarse.

She flinches, her hands jerking away from me. And I all wanted was to take back those words. I wondered if she ever felt the same.

"Ryosuke onichan is outside waiting for you." Were the last words before she slips inside the claustrophobic hospital room, leaving me out on the cold corridor outside.

I ignore her words, descending down the fire emergency stairs and exit from the back door on the ground floor, knowing he would be waiting at the towards the front area of the building.

Doing what I do best, I break into a run. And avoid my issues, again.

Chapter 18 - Ryosuke

New Chapter!!!

Warning: suicide is mentioned within this chapter. Please take care of yourselves and read what is most comfortable for you.

Just another reminder that this chapter is over 3000 words and is on the chunky side of chapters so as per usual, I reccommend reading this one when you have more time to spare. If you could read the chapter till the end, it'll mean a lot to me.

Anyways, enjoy your reading time!!!□□□

"Life is suffering. It is hard. The world is cursed. But you still find reasons to live."

- Princess Mononoke, Studio Ghibli

Babysitting was never a part of my job description but here we were.

"Take that out of your mouth." I said, contemplating on whether I should just tear it away from their mouths.

"It's tabaco. Not weed." Akira retorted, leaning against his motorbike, refusing to take the bud out while Haru and Yuto stuffed theirs away in their pockets. Those two were the most docile of the five but also the most unpredictable when provoked.

"And we're in front of a hospital." I snapped back.

"Since when do you care about that?" Ren quipped while others snickered.

"Since there are newborns and children. Take it out."

Begrudgingly, they either crushed the cancer-causing sticks under their boot or placed them away, a frown forming on their faces. They can hate me for all I care but it was my responsibility to make sure they're not on their deathbeds, hacking up blood and tar in their twenties. That was not why I brought them here.

Leaning against my own motorcycle, I go through my phone, answering emails and texting messages to Kaito who was working with my father in my place.

"When are you going to allow us to ride again?" Ren nagged, the rest of them questioning the same.

"You just did."

"Freely?" They all chorused like newborn chicks begging for attention.

"When you understand responsibility."

"Who's she?" Satoru, the most quiet and observant one mouthed, all of our attention directed towards the girl in an oversized grey hoodie, the hood swallowing much of her head and face. Her arms were crossed at her chest as she stalked towards us. Hesitating briefly, glancing over at the kids the same age as her, she shakes her head, releasing a sigh then walks over to stand beside me.

The kids piqued with interest and curiosity, eyes going wide, craning their necks to see the girl but made no move to do anything knowing better.

Hikari doesn't greet me as usual, only remaining silent.

She was probably the only kid I would tolerate with her brazen if not rude behaviour. She wasn't always this hard to deal with but when life is far from comfortable, you were bound to toughen up. It was a matter of survival.

"I'm scared." She muttered, still looking ahead her body locked and rigid. "I'm scared of losing her."

I say nothing. I've never lost parents or siblings - not permanently at least. And I was far from good at comforting those grieving.

The kids sense that this conversation wasn't for their ears to hear and disperse. They were reckless and stupid but not inhumane. They would vehemently disagree but each of them clung to their youth and innocence somewhere within their minds. Though majority was shattered by their parents, relatives, and schoolteachers.

Hikari faces me, unsatisfied with my silence, her brows furrowed and her mouth set with a disapproving frown.

"Not mom," she added, the extra information completing the picture. Having conversations with her was always like working out a puzzle. Most of the time I could work with what I had but at times like these, she had to give all the pieces for me to finish them.

"Me too." I admitted, finding it fair for the both of us to have an honest conversation knowing she rarely likes conversing at all.

"Are you going to disappear again? Like you did before?" she interrogated, leaving a thick trace of distrust.

Her questions take me by surprise. She may only have been a young kid at the time but she wasn't a kid anymore. At least not in society's eyes. And she was far from stupid.

"No. I'm not leaving." I answered.

"Do you swear? Because if my memories serve me right, you said the exact same thing last time. But you still left her." She accused her voice harsh and cold.

I couldn't blame her.

However, I don't regret the choice I made. Should the options appear in front of me again with the same circumstances, I would still stay by my sister's side. I would still leave the States for Japan if Minori asked.

But she doesn't need me anymore, a voice echoed. I'm not needed anymore.

"I swear." I looked her dead in the eye. "I will be here."

Her jaw ticks and I wasn't emotionally intelligent enough to understand why.

"Why did you leave? It can't be as simple as wanting to stay with your family. You hate your father."

It was a well-known secret. My father loathes and I dislike him just as much. But we both deal with each other's presence because there was no choice but to. I resent him. For being one of the reason I was alive. For providing a life I wanted no part in.

For raising me and my sister in two different ways.

"Blood is thicker than water I guess." I replied.

Anger flickers and widens her eyes as she grabs the side of my jacket, pulling me down to meet her face.

"You didn't see her crumble like I did! I watched her fall apart and destroy herself! I watched her be ridiculed and screamed at my mother! I watched her letting our parents do and say whatever they wanted because it didn't matter to her anymore. She just wanted to end and I know she's waiting for the perfect time to finish her life once and for all! So how dare you vow to me you will be here when you know you'll choose your family over her!" Her voice becomes hoarse as rage filled tears mixed with guilt spill from her eyes that were so similar to her sister.

"Listen to me well Hikari." I cautioned. "I do not regret the choice I made. Just as much as you care about your sister, I care about mine. If she asks to leave with me, I leave. If she tells me to die with her, I do."

Confusion clashes with understanding as her grip on my jacket loosens.

"I have made a promise with you and I will follow through with it," I continued. "I will stand by your sister's side and I will not let her die."

She nods. I assume it was more to herself than to show me she understood but it didn't matter. She inhales deeply, and exhales, swallowing deeply she shoves her hand back into the pocket of her hoodie, retrieving several pieces of paper and hands them over to me.

Murderer's daughter.

Go kill yourself.

We're after you. There's no use in hiding.

Traitor.

If you don't surrender to the Oyabun I will kill you myself.

The content written were childish at best and yet an irritating sense of annoyance and ire flows through me. It was unlikely for men in the organization to write these since the vast majority were simple minded and would just say their threats to their faces and deal with the consequence of disagreeing with the Oyabun's choices which were akin to treason.

"I know they're empty threats but I don't want them to be seen by her." Hikari's voice forces me to return my attention back to her. "It'll just become another motive for her to die."

"You did well." I commend. "I'll find out who's behind it."

"You will stop it right?"

"I'll be doing more than that."

She doesn't push for the unsend words and offers a small smile. It was her way of saying thanks and I accepted it. Turning on her heels on the gravel ground, she walks back into the direction of the hospital and to her mother.

"They look nothing alike." Ren commented after a while, the lot returning back.

"Just because they're siblings, doesn't mean they have to look like twins." Akira grimaced, shoving his hands in the pocket of his ripped jeans.

Looking above the cloudless sky with a blank stare, Satoru offered, "They have the same eyes."

"But they are two completely different people." Haru agreed with Ren. "One's nice. The other chooses who to be nice to."

"I respect her." Akira said, slinging his right arm over Yuto's shoulder. "Women who don't bend. Strong personalities. Like boss' sister. Minori-san is one hell of a woman."

I would have broken his finger or two for saying my sisters name so easily if I had not seen Kaya dashing on the other side of the carpark, away from where we agreed to meet. She had her head down, her dark brown hair flying everywhere as she runs across the road and away from the hospital grounds.

It wasn't unexpected per say but it does throw plans and agreements. Schedules. Timing. Lists.

Ignoring the kids shouts, I run after her, hearing her haggard breathing before grabbing her wrist and yanking her close to me.

A screams tears from her, sharp and concerning as she struggles against my hold only alarming me all the more. Using both my hands, I grab her shoulders, bony even underneath the layers of clothes and shook her to gain her attention.

"Kaya, talk to me," I demanded.

"No, no, no," she wailed, shaking her head. Her face was blotchy, her eyes red as she struggled to breathe, each inhale getting caught in her throat and lungs.

What the fuck did her mother tell her now?

I bring her body closer to me and hold her tight and she continued to mutter the same word in denial- of what? I wasn't sure.

She had more invaders in her mind than I've ever had. Problems and adversity finds her when all she wants is peace. Silence even.

Loosening my hold on her, I tried again, "Kaya, talk to me."

"I . . . I . . ." she trailed off. "I'm exhausted."

She chose to omit the truth.

But I don't push.

"Then let's go home."

Unease invade my system as I observe Kaya from the inside.

She sits on a wooden outdoor chair in the balcony overlooking the unending mountain full of trees, her back slumped, her face blank. She hasn't spoken to me for the past four hours pleading to be left alone.

I contemplated whether to bring her here or back to the main house but she insisted to not go back to the main house. That concerned me more.

Faking a smile and making small talk was an unfortunate talent she had. If she couldn't do that in front of Mom, there was something in her mind that was draining her. Stealing away her strength. Eating away the little energy she has.

Four hours is enough for alone time.

Getting up from the couch, I pour water in the kettle and switch it on. Grabbing two mugs from the cupboard, I retrieve two teabags and place one in each mug and wait for the water to boil. Mindlessly tapping the kitchen counter, I direct my attention back to her, finding her face lifted, staring at the sky.

Nearing night, the sky was washed with an array of colors, though shades of orange and red dominates most. Rayleigh scattering - a process in which molecules like nitrogen and oxygen in different sizes scatter rays of the sun into separate wavelengths which in turn appear as different colors to our eyes.

The kettle clicks and I pour the water into the mugs. Grabbing a light blanket with the tea filed mugs, I slide the balcony door open. She doesn't acknowledge me or react, keeping her gaze on the sky that begins to darken into navy as the stars reappear.

Placing my own mug on the small table, I place the other mug in her hands, making sure she actually holds onto them and not burn her hands like she did the other time. She does although her attention remains fixed to the sky.

Unfolding the blanket, I wrap it around her thin frame before settling on the chair next to her.

"Rayleigh scattering," she mumbled before looking down at her mug. "Evening twilight. A finite amount of time between sunset and dusk. When the sky is neither totally lit nor totally dark."

Inhaling and exhaling deeply, she runs her fingers on the rim of her mug before blowing gently and takes a sip of it. Something similar to relief fills me.

A faint smile paints her face before she whispers, "Rosemary tea. Contains antioxidant, anti-inflammatory and antimicrobial properties."

Being academically number one was one thing she was obsessed with, hence why the abundance in knowledge. But the other obsession was tea. I could still remember her collecting dried tea leaves and placing them into small jars, organizing them in alphabetical order by name.

"Ryo look!" she squealed, pulling on my arm and dragging me inside her room.

I never changed the layout of my room but she does any moment she decides she should. Minori also rearranges her room in the middle of the night because she felt like it but I still couldn't understand why that's necessary.

Her bed with light purple sheets that was in the centre of the right-side wall was now pushed to the left-hand corner of the room next to her window while a shelf filled with jars with a sticker and names replaced the bed. I knew they were tea leaves, mom taught me a basic range and how to prepare them. But there were more than my knowledge branched out to.

"This is my new collection," she said triumphantly, letting go of my arm and grabbing one of them. Unscrewing the lid, she inhales deeply before shoving it right underneath my nose. "Smell it."

It smelt like other teas. Earthy, musky and a little sweet.

"This is lotus tea." She screws the lid and puts in my hand. "It supposedly helps with brain function, improve memory and can help with sleep." She grins and her honeycomb eyes sparkle against the sunlight seeping though her window.

From that day, I asked Mom to teach me a new tea every day and committed them to memory. I wanted to know everything she knew. I wanted to understand everything she had to say. I wanted to know everything about her.

I was so certain I knew her. That I knew what she knew and understood what she said.

But I don't.

I don't know what she knows. I don't know what her words mean, what her body language means, what all her reasons are in suppressing or faking emotions. I don't know her.

"Three times." She mumbled out of the blue. "Always in group of three."

I give her a questioning look.

"You tap your fingers three times. Then wait. Then tap three times again. Most people tap with their fingers over and over. No intervals. No waiting. You're a control freak even without thinking."

"And you're not?"

"Not like you."

"You used a ruler to measure the distance between the jars you collected so that they we were all even. You weighed each jar so they all had the same amount of tea in them. You insisted on writing on the boards in school because other people's handwriting was uneven and unreadable. You volunteer to be in leadership roles in schools because you need all events occurring in school to run time and on schedule. And you're not a control freak?"

"Okay, maybe I was. But I don't do that anymore." She takes another sip of her tea.

"You send a message to your sister every morning exactly at 7 o'clock before school starts and another one 8 o'clock at night even when you're both under the same roof because if you don't get the chance to talk to her, you at least communicated through text. You always arrive where you need to be right on the dot because you think you can't be a second late."

"You say that as if you don't check in on your sister every day. I know you do something similar."

I do, but I say nothing.

Gripping onto her mug tight, her eyes wander, blinking rapidly.

"What am I to you?" She asked, tone soft, her eyes reddening, tears building, her mouth trembling.

"You are my person."

"What does that mean?"

"Someone I protect." I answered before taking a sip of my own tea.

A tear falls. I hated it.

"Is that akin to responsibility?"

Another tear cascades down her cheek, dropping onto the wooden floor. My jaw ticks.

"Yes." I place my mug down.

"Because you've known me for a long time." She said, closing her eyes, tears from both her eyes falling.

"Because I decided you're important." I rephrased her words. She wasn't wrong. But her thoughts did not encompass the full reason. Not even by a margin.

"Like a friend?"

"No." I said.

She opens her eyes, a swirl of emotions running through them though I couldn't figure out what emotions they were.

"A friend is someone you mutually agree to like." I continued. "You enjoy their company, the time spent with them. What I feel for you is not friendship."

"Then what?"

"I don't think there's a word for it."

"Describe it to me then."

"When I see you smile, it's the only expression that sticks on my mind. When I see you cry, the world seems to dull and cave in. When I see you eat and drink and enjoy your meal, a weight I didn't know existed seems to lift from my system. When someone hurts you regardless of their intentions, I have the abrupt urge to obliterate them. And when you laugh . . ." I trailed off.

Running away from Kaito who was chasing us in a game of tag, the new girl squeals scared of being tagged but she was too happy to care.

Her smile creased the side of her eyes, and the light brown color of it shined in the warm sunshine. I've only known her for . . . I don't know. Not very long. And yet, she glowed. Warm and bright.

"You're glowing." I finished off.

Her cheeks were flushed, eyes more red than they were minutes before, and she was hitching with every inhale and exhale. Her hands shook, sloshing the tea inside the mug as those caramel brown eyes glistened from the tears.

Rising from my place, I take the mug out of her hands and scoop her frame and resettle ourselves in her chair. I couldn't understand the reasoning behind her tears but I hated them anyway. Tears were only shed in extreme low emotions and I hated that on her.

Besides from protecting her and keeping her alive, I've decided to add another agender onto my list.

Make her smile more often.

Chapter 19 - Ryosuke

T hick scarlet liquid seeps into her drenched clothes as her face drains away in color, seconds ticking by. Her radial pulse begins to weaken, fading though it was beating faster than it should, trying to compensate the loss of oxygen in the body. The rise and fall of her chest is rapid but faint like the climax of a music before it fades and silences completely.

No, that will not happen.

Pressing down firmly with a thick towel pressed on her neck, traces of her blood already beginning ooze through, I scoop her weightless frame into my arms, my own heart beating erratically in my chest as the thought of losing her smothers me, beginning the process of suffocation around my own neck. Its hold on me tightened with every second passing by.

Her skin is cold to the touch, the fucking grim reaper no doubt hovering over us as I race myself down the entrance of the ED, health staff appearing by my side in seconds, prying her body away from me.

And I already felt like I lost a part of her.

Letting her go was the last thing I wanted to do. But if I kept her to me, she wouldn't survive.

They steal her away from me and rush her into the treatment room, nurses coming in out in a run, grabbing medical supplies, blood transfusions, and doctors – urgency and gravity of the situation unmistakeable.

I pace back and forth in front of the treatment room as I willed my hands to stop fucking shaking. I fist them, my nails digging into my palm. But I felt no pain, nor reprieve. Like the blood soaking her clothes, terror and panic spread through my system as a poison with no antidote, and no cure, killing me slowly and effectively.

Minutes tick by with no information, no update.

No news is good news I tell myself. No news is good news. No news is good news.

"Sir. Sir!"

I snap my attention to the man in navy blue scrubs with a cap covering the top of his head, eyes drooped as he assessed me from top to bottom.

"How is she?" I asked, my voice coming out as a whisper sounding nothing like me.

"We did the best we could," he pauses, eyes solemn. "However, unfortunately she could not make it. Too much blood was lost and the damage to the veins and arteries were irreparable. I am sorry for your loss."

Loss. Loss? Loss, the word echoed.

No. I shake my head. No. No.

My arm desperately reaches out towards her, landing on nothing but an empty pillow. The other side of the bed where she should have been was empty and cold.

"Kaya?!" I yelled into the dark, my voice echoing against the walls, drifting elsewhere in the house. Only silence answer my calls.

Hurling myself out of the bed, I continue to yell for her name, my eyes frantically trying to find her long black hair, light brown eyes, smooth pale skin. Blood pumps harsh in my ears, deafening me and voice.

"Kaya!"

Banging open all and every door, I go in and out of the unlit rooms, finding each of them vacant and empty. With every room I enter not finding her, the more irrational thoughts surge my mind with retribution.

She's gone. She left, disappeared.

She's dead.

I rush back into the living room, demanding the fucking voices in my head to shut the hell up.

She is not dead, I tell myself. She is fine. She is alive.

Cool autumn wind blows brushing against my skin spotted with sweat, providing a reprieve from overheating body.

Wind? I closed all the windows and doors. Safety was not something I messed with.

My eyes drift to the think curtain lazily flowing with the wind, the sliding door leading to the backyard. I immediately pace myself over, leading myself out.

Relief floods within me as I continue to close the distance between her.

Her inky thick long black hair drift gently against the wind as her dazed eyes stare into the moonlit night sky. It was a full moon tonight, it's light glimmering a hazy glow both haunting and stupendous.

"Kaya?" I called out, my hand reaching for hers.

She doesn't respond. She doesn't even look my way; her gaze continue to stare at the moon. Or the stars.

"Kaya." I called out for her again, a little louder.

No response. But she smiles, free and large, crinkling the side of her eyes.

Kaya was always beautiful. A natural Asian beauty with pale clear skin, V-shaped face, double lid big brown eyes and full pink lips. However, her natural beauty couldn't be encased within beauty standards. It was the cute way she pouts her lips when she wants something and knows she will get it. It was the funny way she scrunches her nose when it's clear she doesn't want what was happening and communicates without saying a single word. It was her earth gem-like eyes that glints and dazzles from fascination, wonder, and awe. Like now.

"So pretty," she whispered before her gaze meets mine.

Her eyes were full of life. And yet, it seemed distant. So far away from reality. Tilting her head, she closes the space between us.

"Kenji?" she laughed under her breath, her tone clear and silk like. "You'll catch a cold. You need to wear something warmer."

A weight drops, sinking me down below. My hand on her tightens but she doesn't react.

Her unoccupied hand reaches for my face, palming the side of my cheek.

"You've grown so much taller." She mused, sounding almost like a praise.

With the initial desperation of needing to find her settling, the reels in my psyche turn with intended purpose, realising it was only a few days away until Kenji's death anniversary and birthday. It would make sense if longing heightens for her during this period of time. Especially given that she's been in a constant state of distress and restlessness.

She won't remember any of this I knew. Sleepwalking and talking wasn't something I was entirely familiar with but I doubted she would recall any of it. Confronting her with reality wouldn't serve any purpose in this moment.

Don't hurt her. Don't overwhelm her. Don't corner her.

Make her smile. Make her happy. Make her want to stay.

"Yeah, I did." I replied, agreeing with her current thoughts. She nods gleefully, her smiles brightening all the more. "And you're right, it is cold. Let's go inside, I want to get warm."

"Okay," she easily complies, letting me lead the way. I don't loosen my hold on her. The idea of her disappearing in front of me still too raw.

As we reached closer towards the doors, her grip on my hand loosens and I turn around just in time to catch her as her body to give way and her eye lids close. Out of fear or instinct, I bring my fingers to the carotid pulse point and measure her pulse and monitor her breathing. Everything was within normal range, only indicating that she stopped sleepwalking and fell into deep sleep but my mind refused to agree with logic.

Picking her up into my arms, feeling for the rise and fall of her chest and listening to her soft snore, I return back to our room and place her underneath the comforter, letting myself lie down next to her.

I didn't sleep for the rest of the night.

Clicking against the small letters of the laptop keyboard typing away whatever code she was doing, she finally clicks enter before the whole screen illuminates with both familiar and unfamiliar names with suspicious activity through their choice in technological device

"Are any of them familiar?" she questioned, scrolling down slowly for me to read the names.

I wasn't surprised these people thought it'd be safe to steal away our profits given that they only withdraw insignificant amounts that could be ignored. However, I was surprised to see the sheer number of individuals or perhaps they were a formed pact, to lay their hands on wealth they had no part in earning.

It was almost pitiful if it weren't equally pathetic.

"Wait, look at this," she beckons me to come closer, her subtle water lily scent drifting into my senses. She did have a classic, boring vanilla scent phase which I did not like at all but now that she was back to subtle fine scents, my olfactory system was pleased.

Instead of looking at the screen, I look at her. Dressed in my top and her jeans from yesterday she looked comfortable and well put. Unlike her usual hair tied back into a ponytail that drifted down her back, today, her hair was neatly tied into one singular plait. It was her favorite hair updo when she was five years old, freshly entering school. She was constantly shouting that she felt like a princess.

Pulling away my attention from her to the screen, email correlation between two men who are known to cause trouble when they saw fit shone on the screen.

23:47pm

Daisuke

Report to me when you're finished.

03:11am

Hanzo

Mission accomplished. Reward?

03:18am

Daisuke

Good. With what we have gained, we can initiate the next round.

Meet us at our usual place three nights from today.

That was sent two days ago, meaning tomorrow night, these two and possibly more of them would be in the same room celebrating whatever victory they have succeeded in. Cheers will be shared, comments will be made, and pretentious bragging would be said. Pity they got ahead of themselves and rushed their whole plan.

A smirk forms my face. Ruining fun and causing misfortune were entertaining.

"What do you plan to do?" Kaya asked, turning her head to face me, her lips left parted, eyes wide and doe like. "You are going to stop it right?"

An amusing thought passes by.

"We are going to stop it." I rephrased her words.

"We?" Her right brow dips down. "Wait it's not what I'm think right?"

"I don't know. What were you thinking?"

"You know exactly what I'm thinking." Her voice rises in volume, annoyance beginning to bleed through.

"Indulge me."

"You want me to stop it. To uh . . ." her eyes wanders. "Finish them."

"Only if you wanted to. I won't stop you." An image of her clicking a gun to one of their heads surfaces my mind and I immediately stored it. It was a satisfying sight, if not spectacular.

"This is a challenge, isn't it?"

"A never said it was. You did." I pointed out, turning around and leaning on the desk.

She crosses her arms, getting defensive. Her eyes burn with a mixture of distaste and interest, both at war with each other. I wait to watch which emotion wins.

"This has nothing to do with me."

"No, it doesn't." I agreed. "Unless we go in detail. Then anything involved within the organization we exist in will involve you."

Involve the both of us my mind thought.

She bites the inside of her cheeks and I pull on her cheeks to stop it.

"What are you doing!" She yelled but I couldn't give a fuck.

"If you need to hurt something, hurt me! I don't care if you want rip open my skin or tear it apart but you will stop doing that. Do you understand?"

She pulls back. From surprise or from fear I did not know. I could only hope it wasn't from the latter.

Don't hurt her. Don't overwhelm her. Don't corner her.

Make her smile. Make her happy. Make her want to stay.

"Sorry. I didn't mean to yell." I began to say not knowing how apologising actually worked. With Minori a simple look and she would understand.

With Kaito he could tell with my actions. With Kaya looks, actions, and words were all important. "I just . . . I just don't like seeing you hurt yourself."

"And you prefer me hurting you?" She asked in a whisper.

"Yes."

"And if we switched roles? Do you think I'll like that?" She sounded hurt and I was failing at all the words I've been chanting in my head.

The mere thought of inflicting harm on her makes me want to kill myself. Burn myself alive, sever all limbs and lodge the weapon deep into my chest, I don't care.

"I can't promise anything," she admits, balling her fists. "But I can promise I'll try."

I nod in understanding. That was more than I could ask from her right now.

"Thank you."

She smiles and immediately changes the subject. "I'm hungry."

Sighing, I nod. Aware that this subject is dropped, we both leave the room and head towards the kitchen.

Ignorance was not a bliss. Ignorance was still ignorance.

But perhaps such idea was created out of necessity. Because it created a barrier in awareness, protecting us even if it was temporary.

However, once the veil is taken away, reality was bound to inflict pain.

It was only a matter of when. Feel the unbearable pain now or later?

Usually, I preferred now rather than later. But now I was quickly changing to the latter. Later. Always later.

Chapter 20 - Kaya

Now Chapter!!! ..... and some action time

Parked out of sight in front of a luxurious grey-white mansion on the costal side of town was not how I thought I would be spending my Friday night.

The waves were unusually calm tonight, and only slapped against the nearshore sandbars in a half-heartedly manner. Wind was oddly non-existent creating an eery feel to this potentially awful night.

Everything was too still. Too calm. Too artificial.

For a crazy moment, perhaps in another dimension of the world, I could have sworn Ryo was the one who decided all of this. To make everything artificially perfect.

It was after all, his favourite way to play with people's feelings before ending their lives and chucking their corpses in a ditch designated for new construction plans. There was no denying that underneath each and every single building the Sakurazuki construction group was responsible for, housed at least a dozen bodies built on top of them. It was the most cost effective, efficient, and easiest method of disposing them.

No one checks. No one looks. And most importantly, no one is bold enough to question.

"Didn't think you'd be joining. And here I thought you can only make flower arrangements look pretty." Kaito commented, leaning against the hood of his car.

If that comment came from anyone else, I would be hurling my fist into their sternums but from Kaito it didn't matter. I knew and understood he was only making a joke to calm me down. My nerves were obvious and for an empath and another control freak like Kaito, he just needed to do something about it.

"Wasn't my idea of fun either." I replied, crossing my arms to stop my hands from shaking. "I was forced rather than joined."

"No forcing or coercion was done. You chose to be here." Ryo corrected, looking up from his tablet before opening the car door to chuck it away. The sleeve of his dress shirt strained with the muscle mass that packed underneath with every movement and I couldn't seem to look away.

Kaito catches where my attention was and wiggled his brows up and down. I gave him the finger to which he replied with a cackling laugh, leaving Ryo confused.

Confused Ryo was hands down, one of the most interesting facial expression he owned. Possibly also the most expressive he becomes. His right brow dips low, and his dark brown eyes harden, creasing at the sides but not in a frightening way. More like disgusted way.

It was damn hilarious.

And Kaito laughed harder.

While I put on a neutral, 'I have no idea what he is laughing at' face.

Ryo sighs and closes his eyes, as though he was a fed-up father who gave up on talking sense to his children.

Well, he kind was like that to the five kids who have been surprisingly well behaved all of yesterday and today. They were like any teenage boys who were always lured into some kind of mischief, constantly chasing for that adrenaline high. Whether that was beating each other half to death, riding their motorcycles close to death or annoying Ryo to their graves.

They were far from innocent but still, their innocence shines through when they look at Ryo. They may mock him, antagonize him, and irritate him but when you see them, their eyes flash with admiration and ease. Something I knew were rare occurrences for teens like them who were regularly denied a safe place or safe people to go to.

Ryo was a safe place. He was a safe person.

Well, he was only safe to people he granted safety. Not the people inside the mansion with golden lit rooms and on trend music blasting from it.

"We're allowed to beat them up right?" Akira asked, genuinely excited for what laid ahead. Akira with his bleached blond, brown hair was more or less the leader of the group. The one who calls the shots. Not my idea of a leader but the boys followed him without question.

Three out of the five boys decided to join while the other two were back at home base to deliver any new information that may arise. To put it simply, two real adrenaline junkies plus one quiet but lethal child was here while the two cute nerdy kids assisted in a strategic manner. Adrenaline junkies don't think far ahead for strategy anyway.

"You can kill to your heart's desire." Kaito replied, ruffling Akira's head. Akira swats him away. "Just not the three we have our eyes on."

"Really?" Rens eyes widen like a puppy given his treat. Ren was the life of a party. Always seeking some kind of thrill. He was laid back and generally speaking welcoming but there was certainly something off about him that unnerved people. I still couldn't quite pinpoint what.

"Yep. Half an hour of controlled beating. You can do whatever you like. Just no hitting women or children if there are any. The men are all yours."

"Yes!" Ren beamed while Akira smirked in creepy delight.

"What do we do if there are children? Letting them see us beating their parents could hardly be called merciful." Satoru spoke up with a detached stare.

"Trauma is part of growing up on this side of the world. Call it education." Kaito said with a shrug. Akira and Ren hacked a laugh. Satoru shook his head. Ryo simply sighed.

"Are we ready or is the matter going to resolve itself by the time you are?" Ryo remarked with disappointment.

"We were born ready Boss." Ren quipped with a big smile.

"Then go." He said and we all spread to where we were stationed to be.

By the time Ryo, Kaito and myself entered the mansion, the whole of third floor where the party was held was pure chaos. Blood splattered the marbled floors, walls, ceilings, while champaign and wine glasses were shattered and splintered creating hazard on the ground.

Thankfully there were no children in attendance and all the women that the eye could see were taken out held as hostage elsewhere.

Our men plus the three kids were already pressing their necks onto the glass littered floors, confiscating their right to breathe as well as making them bleed in the process. Akira and Ren found entertainment in throwing blows after blows into their faces and abdomen, watching them crumble and lose conscious from the pain. Satoru on the other hand did thing with more finesse, striking them with one blow to knock them out or . . . may have potentially killed them. Couldn't tell for sure.

Shrills and screams howled from all directions and men attempted to flee with genuine fear laced onto their face. But even if they managed to swerve their way out, up or down, our men surrounded the whole place. The chances of getting out unharmed were very close to zero.

"There." Kaito pointed to a wall that seemed . . . just like a normal wall.

Ryo doesn't questions and walked leisurely towards the wall, cocking his head to one side, examining. His eyes scanned the entirety of the wall from right to left. Left to right. His attention diverts, picking up an antique porcelain vase that had probably fallen when our men burst in and placed it back onto the table that was placed only for show.

I was surprised it didn't have a single crack.

"I see." Ryo muttered before he sank his arm inside the vase and the wall groaned pulling upwards. A heinous smile decorated Kaito and Ryo's face as the lifting wall revealed the three men we were finding, all scrambled on the floor with their guns all aimed at Ryo. He doesn't take notice and takes a step forward.

"H-how did you know?" Hanzo stuttered, his voice quivering before he swallowed deeply. He was a bald, bald man who I assume had the same amount of brain cells as the hair he had on his head. None.

"You underestimate us." Ryo said taking another step, crouching down right in front of Hanzo who's gun was pressed onto Ryo's forehead. My stomach squeezes with apprehension while my mind screamed for him to get away. But logic understood Ryo knew what he was doing.

Mind games. Let them think they have control. Power.

"You know, we trusted you. You weren't so bad." Ryo continued tone almost seemingly genuine as he gripped Hanzo's arm, lowering down his gun. He doesn't resist, letting Ryo command his body and mind. "I'll give you a choice. You can come out clean and repent. Painful but honourable." Hanzo's eyes spark with hope. "Or make everything unnecessarily complicated. Your call."

There would be no repenting. Once he comes out clean, death would be waiting for them. There was no honor in betraying the organization. That I knew.

"Don't listen to him!" Katsu yelped as his eyes wandered over to Kaito and I. Like he had chosen his target he aimed the gun towards me. "I'll kill her!"

"Then do it." Ryo challenged, not taking his eyes away from Hanzo. "I dare you."

His finger shook against the trigger. I smiled.

Weak.

Sweeping out my own gun from the back pocket of my pants I aim and pull the trigger. A loud bang fills the room, the bullet beautifully penetrating through Katsu's right shoulder, jerking his body before crashing down on to his right side, his gun clattering towards Kaito who retrieves with a proud smile.

"Wild." Kaito clapped his hands with an approving smile. "Who knew you were ruthless?"

"A woman can be many things." I said, walking over towards Katsu who was out cold already. Most people would be howling in pain. He was so weak he lost conscious. At least he was smart enough to know none of them would leave alive.

"Indeed." Kaito agreed nodding his head.

"I-I surrender!" Hanzo exclaimed a beat later, both his arms in the air as his face paled another shade lights, perspiration dripping down his forehead. On the other hand, a lazy smile paints over Ryo's face.

"Excellent. You've made the right dec-"

I topple over him as another bullet shoots past us. Eyes closed, heart racing, breaths mingling, I exhale deeply in genuine relief before I scramble off of him to find Kaito already incapacitating Daisuke who attempted to shoot down Ryo.

That was unexpected. Daisuke was quiet throughout and from what I knew, only knew how to take orders. Not the kind to initiate action on his own. I guess he wasn't just a marionette puppet.

"You promised me!" Ryo shook my body with his hands grasping tightly on my shoulders. His eyes blazed with a hint of shock, anger, and fear. "You promised you wouldn't try doing anything that could harm you!

Anger bloomed inside. Why was he lecturing me? Why was he angry?

"And let you bleed out to death? No! I'm not apologising for what I did. I saved you!" I screamed back at him yanking his arms away from me. "And I'm fine!"

"No you're not!" He roared, grabbing my arm and brings it closer to my eyes. "What do you call that?"

The fabric of my sleeves were frayed a gash dripping blood, spreading around the edges of the sleeves, drenching it.

I was in such an adrenaline high I couldn't feel the pain. Even after realising, I still couldn't.

"Oh," was all I could manage to say. Anger dissipated as wonder barged in. Being observant was one thing. How was he able to see the things I couldn't?

"Love's spat?" Kaito joked looking down on the both of us.

"Don't be ridiculous." Ryo dismissed before he started dishing out orders. "Get them tied up and restrained. Take them wherever you see fit and get answers before I get there."

"Yeah, yeah, yeah. I get it." Kaito said stepping away from us as he began to bark orders at the men who seemed like they already finished beating the crap out of every man who were affiliated with the three pathetic men in front of us.

"Let me look." He wraps his hand a few inches away from the wound and inspects it.

"It's a small gnash. Nothing major." I said. He only gives an exasperated look.

Taking out a handkerchief, he wraps it around the wound. "Press on it hard. Don't let go until we get back."

He stands back up, joining Kaito to give more orders to his men and lectures to the kids who all had a wolfish grin, no doubted delighted with tonight's activities. One by one they begin to filter out, some kicking hard behind the legs of now prisoners while others simply dragged the unconscious bodies.

Mind blank and unsure of what I should be doing, I just sat on the floor staring.

Only now the wound begins to sting and throb.

I hated this battle scar already.

Chapter 21 - Kaya

It's not that I condone torture or murder – okay maybe I do, depending on who – but there was something so exhilarating and fascinating watching a person who knew what they were doing so well they can make torture appear like art.

"Wrong answer."

Another finger hacked off.

Another gruelling scream.

Once Hanzo exclaimed to surrender, I was certain he would spill everything that we needed to know but the man was tougher than I gave credit for. If he had been just as loyal to the Sakurazuki organization as he did for whatever and whoever he was devoted to, he would have been a valued member.

Pity he chose the wrong side.

Sakurazuki-gumi was patient. But they were not merciful.

Hanzo gasped every breath; his chest rose high and fell deep as though he was never able to breathe in as much as his body wanted. The smell of his sweat and blood permeated this stifling cellar room close to a construction site that was soon to operate to construct a new business high rise building.

Ironic to think that the corpses of old-fashioned minded people were going to become a foundational layer for a building created to nurture and employee modern, forward minded people.

"It's a pity. I thought we both came to a conclusion together." Kaito drawled pacing between Hanzo and Katsu. Daisuke was thrown into a cellar of his own with Ryo to keep him company. I would have asked what they were doing, or rather what Ryo was intended on doing to him, but I kept my mouth shut – I wasn't quite certain whether I wanted to know.

"There . . . t-there would be n-no point." Hanzo heaved from his seat. Strapped securely onto a wooden chair, each of his legs were bounded onto the front to legs of the chair, digging raw into in his flesh while his arms were bounded on each arm rest. In the past hour, he has lost three fingers: two pinkies and his right thumb.

"Perhaps not for you, but I am sure you are intelligent enough to know that your admission can assist other people as well as doing yourself a favor." Kaito turned his attention onto Katsu who sat opposite Hanzo. "Don't you agree?"

Katsu swallowed hard but said nothing – actually he couldn't say a word given that his mouth was sealed shut with masking tape. His nose flared with each exhale, his chest rising quicker than what could count has regular or normal but there was a pleasure in watching people who deserve suffering, suffer. No hard feelings for them but I needed this release. Call it another bad habit – and a terrible personality and shit morals – but fuck it, I already had plenty of those. One more couldn't hurt.

"Slow progress?"

I flinch like I had been the one with the hacked off fingers and I could have sworn that my neck muscle pulled out on itself from how fast I snapped to look behind. But there he was, donning on another perfectly clean, pristine suit, arms crossed and blocking the doorway.

I kid you not that door was shut and I am quite certain that I didn't hear anything opening or creaking. And yet, the gated door was wide open. If they weren't bounded, beaten, and missing a couple of fingers, that open door would have been the perfect escape route.

A shame that life was depleting from their eyes by the minute.

"More like no progress." Kaito answered with an amused grin. I have no idea what that means.

"Hm. Pity."

Ryo walked over to table in front of me, displayed with a selection knives and torture tools that I had no idea how to use or what they're called. He hovered his hand above the tools, stopping and picking up the . . . scalpel?

"Well then, might as well use your body for educational purposes."

"E-e-educational purposes?" Katsu stuttered; his face and lips blanched cyan.

Ryo put the scalpel back down, turned around eyeing down Hanzo, then to Katsu. "Educational purposes."

Plastic rubbing against skin pierced through the silence as Ryo donned on a pair of gloves, the scalpel with one hand, a chair with another, its legs scrapping against the concrete floor, closer and closer to the sinners. The chair screeched to a stop in front of Katsu and he began to squeal and whimper, squirming in his bounded seat.

"There are about 34 muscles in the hands and more than 100 ligaments and tendons to support stabilize the joints. Like most parts of the body, there are many nerves with various functions – including sending pain signals to the brain. Specifically, the thalamus though I doubt you had any interest in human anatomy or physiology. But today will be a good day to learn, no?"

Ryo played around with the scalpel with its shield still on, the blade glinting with the promise of precise incisions while Katsu perspired profusely, creating all kinds of noise as he tried to save himself from what was to come.

With a flick of a finger, the shield came off and the blade sliced across skin, from the tip of the finger to his elbow, blood bubbling up to the surface spilling down with a haunting drip, drip, drip.

Katsu writhed in his seat almost looking like he was seizing or having a fit. He looked more blank than he did five seconds ago with his eyes every now and then lolling back into the abyss. Ryo squashed his face with his hand, stealing back Katsu's attention.

"This is only the beginning," he promised with a sneer. "If you can't take it I will sew you back up and repeat the whole process. Use the little intelligence you have and fess up." Ryo ripped off the tape from his mouth leaving an irritated border pink.

Katsu was hyperventilating at this point, slowly taking a glance at Hanzo who had his eyes shut.

"W-we were told t-that there would be more of a . . . a financial benefit in siding with them. W-with you guys we were underappreciated and overused. Cleaning your dirty business and taking on jobs with very little information. But with them, we were paid well and our whole family was taken care of without having to live like us. I did it for my children and for myself. I wanted a better life than the life you gave."

"Who is 'they'?" Ryo questioned.

"Watanabe-gumi but . . ."

"But?"

"I . . . I don't think it's just them. I think there was something more to it than them."

"What do you know?" Ryo turned to Hanzo with wide eyes and his mouth agape.

"I-I don't know much."

"You don't?" His voice deepened – a touch more sinister.

"Well, I mean I, yes." His voice hitched, his eyes wandered across the room and settled to look down at the ground painted red from his blood. "The Watanabe shook hands with some European group who have more easy access to weaponry. T-that's all I know." Hanzo admitted his eyes shut once again.

"And it has nothing to do with the MeX?"

Hanzo open his eyes and nodded eagerly. "They also wanted to get rid of the MeX."

The blade of the scalpel clinked against the rusty chair, clink, clink, clink.

With an audible sigh, he stood up from his chair and shot both men to their deaths, blood spurting out from them both. Ryo placed back the scalpel where it belonged, took off his gloves, dumping them in the trash can beside the door and walked out without a glance, his pristine white shirt now splotched, pink on his sleeves.

In this moment I realised, I have fallen for a man who didn't think twice about killing or death. He had no emotions attached. No feelings. None. He did what was necessary for the organization he was born in, raised in, breathed in, lived in. And he did that without a single flaw.

Because that was what was drilled into his mind, his thought process. To aim well, perfectly, and according to circumstance. To think fast, to think through. To act with information and not with emotions latched on.

He and I were part of the same organization but we lived contrasting lives.

He had responsibilities and duties that would bound him for hell. And I wanted to follow. Like he was the north magnetic pole I desperately wanted to attach with my south.

How messed up was that.

"Kaya, let's go." Kaito said waiting for me by the door.

I take another look at the now dead bodies strapped onto their chairs and hoped it wouldn't stay on my mind – or at least not for long –and following Kaito out the door.

Chapter 22 - Ryosuke

My mind wouldn't shut down.

It was wishful thinking to hope that I could, but I would do anything to remove and eliminate all my memories right now. The sharp scent of blood slowly spreading and staining her lose fitted clothes, eyes rolled to the back of her head, cyanosis of the lips and fingertips as the rise and fall of her chest become more shallow, more rapid until you think you can't hear breath sounds at all.

The weight of each limb, limp and heavy.

And then, I loose rationality. I'm throwing objects; pen and paper from my desk, documents, files, laptops, phones, they all collide against the wall and ricochet back fractured and broken apart. I'm smashing my fists against the mirrors, the glass digging, slicing apart my skin. I'm yelling my throat raw and I can't stop. I physically cannot stop.

"Onichan?"

My attention snaps. Just a foot away from the door outside my room, Minori stood, hands gripping on the doorknob, knuckles pale white. She stares me down intently, gauging out what is playing inside my head – a talent she developed growing up.

"Yeah?" I answered, motioning for her to come inside. Her hands slowly slipped away from the door, before padding inside my room. Just like she always did, ever since she was old enough to walk on her own, she took her seat on the edge of my bed. I bring my chair closer over to her. "What's wrong? Did the Russian idiot offend you? What do you want me to do?"

She gave a half hearted laugh and shook her head. "Nik's fine. I think I'm the annoying one. Didn't think wedding plans could be so exhausting."

"Just get Okasan to help. She'll do everything for you."

"You know I don't want that." Minori grimaced. "I want that day to be my day. I want everything how Nik and I want it. My wedding must be perfect."

I still couldn't believe my sister, my baby sister was getting married in mere months. She was getting married before I was and she had barely explored the world. But her heart was set and so was the heart of the man she was marrying. The simpleness of contentment they exuded when next to each other was disappointingly comforting.

"If you ever decide to cancel the wedding because that Russian idiot decides to be everything he should not, I will finish him."

"Don't you dare." Minori pointed her finger at me. "And even if he did anything he shouldn't be, I will end him. I am more than capable."

That I knew. No need to be told twice.

"Just saying." Shrugging I added, "so, why are you actually here?"

Her body sagged her lips forming a tight line. Her eyes wonder around a short while before they set back on mine. "Kaya called. She said you were acting odd. What happened?"

I raked through my hair with my hand. The thoughts and images in my head were not for sharing. The issues I encounter as part of my job are not her burden. So what do I give up? What worry or problem should I give for her to accept and back away?

"Onichan, stop trying to think of some plausible lie and spit out the truth."

Women were indeed a creature of intuition and I can't seem to get away from them. Particularly this one for the simple reason that she was stubborn. She would never leave without a plausible truth let alone a poorly made up half-truth. This was the girl who stood in front of dear fathers office door until he begrudgingly allowed her to use rifles. She stood there for a total of 4 hours and 53 minutes.

"Kaya almost died, again. And again, I only have myself to blame." I flexed my hands. "I'm going to lose her. I shouldn't . . . I shouldn't be in her life."

My sister doesn't say a word. She blinked once and then pulls my chair closer over to her. "You're being ridiculous." She started, her brows furrowed. "If you leave her, again, who does she have to depend on? Her mother's dying and yes, I know their relationship are strained but she's still her mother. Her sister barely acknowledges her presence and," she places a palm right in front of my face. "I know you like her sister too but let me finish. Kaya doesn't have people who are on her side. If not you then who? If you disappear from her life now, when her life even from the outside looks like it's about to shatter any minute, who's gonna support her?"

If anyone could hate Kaya for valid reasons it was Minori. If Kaya's father hadn't done the things he had, hadn't executed the plans he did, Minori would have lived an entirely different life. This, I had imagined frequently.

Would she have been more naïve? Would she still have picked up a rifle and blade? Would she have like me, shut herself away from the world as a means to protect herself?

The possibilities of such a life were endless. But no amount of pondering, wondering would change reality. Minori was assaulted. Minori knew the ugliness of the world. Minori picked up the rife and blade and finished lives with sophistication, like art.

But Minori learnt to open up. She had always been stronger than I have ever been.

Minori wasn't always close with Kaya. In truth Minori was quite indifferent with her.

Growing up, they were the complete opposite. Minori and I were both reserved. If we didn't need to talk at all, that was luxury. Kaya on the other hand, had no idea when to close her mouth. If she wasn't sleeping or eating, she was chatting away about something absolutely random and irrelevant. Minori found her odd and understandably, bothersome.

Despite that, she was firmly on her side. And now, reprimanding me.

"Do you remember that night I came back and broke apart?" I asked.

A flash of confusion followed by recognition passed by her eyes. She nodded.

"It was her blood on my clothes. And I thought I was going to lose her. Forever." I scoffed a laugh. "That was the first time I think I understood – even partially – what it was like to live in a world where the one person you cared about didn't exist. She was alive and I was going mad."

Minori grabbed my hands and held them tight around hers. "That's normal. It's grief. It's loss." She gave a tight smile. "You try to distract yourself by destroying yourself but deep inside, you know the reality. I've hurt my-self too. I grieved for the stupidly innocent girl that I was before. I wanted her back even though I knew I would never be the same. It's normal, or at least from what I know it is."

Oftentimes, I realise how emotionally more mature she was than me.

She was after all, the first person to protect me from our father.

I exhaled audibly, leaning back against my seat. "Love looks good on you, unfortunately."

"The unfortunately part was unnecessary. But thanks, I like being in love. You should try it too. I'm sure it'll do wonders. Maybe brighten your personality a little." She said shrugging only her right shoulder. "Well, that's all from me. I'm gonna go eat something."

"It's two am."

"So?" She grimaced, looking me up and down. "I'm hungry."

"Is there something on my face?"

"No." I replied without taking my eyes off from her. Something was different. Unlike all the negative different's she had, this was positive. Oddly.

"Then can you stop staring?" Kaya asked but her attitude and tone of voice conveyed the question like a demand and something about that was satisfying.

"No."

"What are you looking for?"

"Something."

"What?"

"I don't know."

"Sorry to interrupt your love staring competition but we've got work to do." Kaito announced, barging himself in between us. I pressed down my foot against his. He grinned in response. "Can't get to work if all we do is stare. Now, who's the likely candidate for this European group we're hutting for?"

"Well there are the Albanians of course," said Kaya swivelling her chair. "but they're a little, you know."

"Barbaric?" Kaito offered.

"Uh, yeah, I guess. Then there are the Irish and the Polish. I just think they're more of a likely candidate but I don't know anything well so. . ."

The Irish and the Polish despise each other so if the Watanabe's truly chose one of the two, they gained yet another foe. But the Polish were weaker in power compared to many so maybe the Irish? But Watanabe had a weird knack for befriending overly aggressive leaders so Albanian's couldn't truly be out of the question.

"Definitely not the Italians or the Russian's?" Kaito questioned looking at me first and then to Kaya. "I mean there's just so many factions."

"There's no need for them to shake hands with Watanabe. There's be no benefit." I answered.

"True. Then I guess we'll do this the old fashioned way? Sit and wait for a while?"

"That sounds boring." Kaya pointed out, her right brow dipping lower than her right.

"It is. But it means I can rest and sleep so actually, it's amazing."

"You make it sound like I work you to death." I noted drily. I do not in fact work him to death. Some later nights? Sure. But I do not force him to do anything and I have never forced him to do said late nights for more than a week straight. He does everything willingly.

"Well done." Kaito smacked a hand on my shoulder. "You perfected the art of describing reality. I should send you a gold star. Kaya, this is revolutionary." He wiped away a fake tear with the theatrical ability of an actor starring in a melodrama musical.

"Careful there." Kaya noted, gently peeling his hand away from my shoulder. "He looks like a human but that is a monster in human skin."

"Oh." Kaito whispered, snapping his attention to Kaya. Dramatically. "You are so right."

Kaya simply nodded. "Let us leave before he eats us alive."

Why on Earth did I trust these two?

Milton Keynes UK
Ingram Content Group UK Ltd.
UKHW031840121024
449535UK00010B/620